THE OUTBACK
MARRIAGE RANSOM

THE OUTBACK MARRIAGE RANSOM

BY

EMMA DARCY

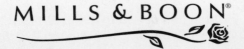

MILLS & BOON®

First published in Great Britain 2004
Large Print edition 2004
Harlequin Mills & Boon Limited,
Eton House, 18-24 Paradise Road,
Richmond, Surrey TW9 1SR

© Emma Darcy 2004

ISBN 0 263 18092 1

Set in Times Roman 17¾ on 19 pt.
16-0804-44140

Printed and bound in Great Britain
by Antony Rowe Ltd, Chippenham, Wiltshire

PROLOGUE

First day at Gundamurra

THE plane was heading down to a red dirt airstrip. Apart from the cluster of buildings that marked the sheep station of Gundamurra, there was no other habitation in sight between here and the horizon—a huge empty landscape dotted with scrubby trees. Ric wished he still had the camera he'd stolen. He could take some unbelievable shots here.

'The middle of nowhere,' Mitch Tyler muttered. 'I'm beginning to think I made the wrong choice.'

'Nah,' Johnny Ellis drawled. 'Anything's better than being locked up. At least we can breathe out here.'

'What? Dust?' Mitch mocked.

The plane landed, kicking up a cloud of it.

'Welcome to the great Australian Outback,' the cop escorting them said derisively. 'And just remember…if you three city smart-arses want to survive, there's nowhere to run.'

All three of them ignored him. They were sixteen. Regardless of what life threw at them, they were going to survive. And Johnny had it right, Ric thought. Six months working on a sheep station, had to be better than a year in a juvenile jail. Ric, for one, couldn't stand overbearing authority. He hoped the guy who ran this place wasn't some kind of tyrant, getting off on having three slaves to do his bidding.

What had the judge said at the sentencing? Something about getting back to ground values. A program that would teach them what real life was about. In other words, you worked to live, not skim off other people. Easy for him to say, sitting behind his bench in a cushy chair, safe with his silver-tailed government income.

There was no *security* in Ric's world.

Never had been.

Thieving what you wanted was the only way to get it. And there was a lot Ric wanted. Though stealing the Porsche to impress Lara Seymour had been stupid. He'd lost her now. That was certain. A girl with her privileged background wouldn't even consider a convicted criminal for a boyfriend.

The plane taxied back to where a guy was waiting beside a four-wheel drive Cherokee. Big guy—broad-shouldered, barrel-chested, craggy weathered face, iron-grey hair. Had to be over fifty but still looking tough and formidable. Not someone to buck in a hurry, Ric decided, though size didn't automatically command his respect. If the guy laid a hand on him...

'John Wayne rides again,' Mitch muttered in the mocking tone he habitually used. Sour on the whole world was Mitch. Could become a real drag, living with him at close quarters.

'No horse,' Johnny remarked with a grin.

He was going to be much easier to get on with, Ric thought.

Johnny Ellis had probably cultivated an affable manner as his stock-in-trade, as well as a protective shield, though he was big enough and strong enough to match anyone in a punch-up. He had friendly hazel eyes, a ready grin, and sun-streaked brown hair that tended to flop over his forehead. He'd been caught dealing in marijuana, though he swore it was only to musicians who'd get it from someone else anyway.

Mitch Tyler was a very different kettle of fish, charged with a serious assault on a guy who, he claimed, had date-raped his sister. Though he hadn't put that defence forward in court. Didn't want his sister dragged into it. He was lean and mean, dark hair, biting blue eyes, and Ric had the sense that violence was simmering under his surface all the time.

Ric, himself, was darker still in colouring. Typical Italian heritage. Black curly hair, almost black eyes, olive skin, with the kind of Latin good looks that attracted the girls. Any girl he wanted. Even Lara. But looks weren't enough in the long run. He had to have money. And all the things money could buy. It was the only way to beat the class difference.

The plane came to a halt.

The cop told them to get their duffle bags from under the back seats. A few minutes later he was leading them out to a way of life which was far, far removed from anything the three of them had known before.

The initial introduction had Ric instantly tensing up.

'Here are your boys, Mister Maguire. Straight off the city streets for you to whip into shape.'

The big old guy—and he sure was big close up—gave the cop a steely look. 'That's not how we do things out here.' The words were softly spoken but they carried a confident authority that scorned any need for physical abuse.

He nodded to them, offering a measure of respect. 'I'm Patrick Maguire. Welcome to Gundamurra. In the Aboriginal language, that means ''Good day.'' I hope you will all eventually feel it was a good day when you first set foot on my place.'

Ric found himself willing to give it a chance.

Fighting it wasn't going to do him any good anyway.

'And you are…?' Patrick Maguire held out a massive hand to Mitch who looked suspiciously at it as though it were a bone-cruncher.

'Mitch Tyler,' he answered, thrusting his own hand out in defiant challenge.

'Good to meet you, Mitch.'

A normal handshake, no attempt to dominate.

Johnny's hand came out with no hesitation. 'Johnny Ellis. Good to meet you, Mister Maguire.' Big smile to the old man, pouring out the charm. Getting onside fast was Johnny.

A weighing look in the steely grey gaze, plus a hint of amusement. No one's fool this, Ric thought, as he himself was targeted by eyes that had probably seen through all the facades people put up.

'Ric Donato,' he said, taking the offered hand, feeling the strength in it, and oddly enough a warmth that took away some of the sense of alienation that was deep in Ric's bones.

'Ready to go?' the old man asked.

'Yeah. I'm ready,' Ric said more aggressively than he meant to.

Ready to take on the whole damned world one day.

And come out on top.

Maybe even win Lara in the end.

He still couldn't get her out of his head. Probably never would. Class...that's what she had. Unattainable for Ric right now but he'd get there. One way or another, he'd make it to where he wanted to be.

CHAPTER ONE

Eighteen years later...

RIC DONATO sat with his executive assistant, Kathryn Ledger, in the Sydney office, checking photographs that had come in, most of them featuring celebrities at the Australian Film Industry Awards. That was the big number this week. Freelance photographers—some reputable, some paparazzi—sent them to his agency via the Internet. His staff sifted through them, choosing the highlights to be sold to magazines around the world.

Always class, Ric reflected with considerable irony. That was what his network of agencies sold—here in Australia, Los Angeles, New York, London, his contacts legion now, all of them eager to jump on his red carpet ride.

The grim realities he'd shot as a photo-journalist covering war zones had won prizes and respect in some quarters but the appeal of those photographs had been very limited. He'd learnt the hard way that it was pretty pictures that sold everywhere. People wanted to see class. They revelled in it, if only vicariously. They turned away from suffering.

Focusing on class had paid off, at both ends of the market. The rich and famous liked his guarantee that nothing negative would be brokered through his agencies. They even alerted his staff about photo op-portunities, happy to supply the demands of the media as long as the shots were positive publicity for them. And the magazines lapped up what he could provide, paying mega-dollars for exclusives.

Everybody happy.

The magic formula for success.

Class…

It was the password to paradise, at least in terms of wealth and acceptability into even the highest social strata. He'd known that instinctively at sixteen, forgotten it in his twenties when he'd pursued other quests, learnt it again in time to build up what had turned into a multimillion dollar business.

Kathryn downloaded yet another photograph from the airport—more Hollywood stars departing, Ric thought, idly watching until one of the faces being revealed galvanised his attention.

Lara?

Her head was ducked down. She was wearing sunglasses. Was that discolouration beside her left cheekbone part of a black eye? Her mouth was puffy as though she'd taken a hit there, as well.

He switched his gaze to the man accompanying her. That was Gary Chappel all right—the guy she'd married—heir and current CEO to the Nursing Home empire his father had built. Born to huge wealth and with the kind of clean-cut handsome looks that could have made him a pin-up model if he'd been so inclined.

But he wasn't looking so attractive in this photo, his mouth thinned into grim lines, hooded eyes emanating a vicious threat. He had one arm wrapped tightly around Lara's shoulders. His other hand had a tight grip on her arm which was tucked between them. Bruisingly tight.

'Wow! There's fodder for the gossip pages,' Kathryn remarked.

Gary and Lara Chappel—definitely an A-list couple in Australian high society, usually photographed as two of the most beautiful people. Ric had seen plenty of shots of them before, but never like this.

'Delete?' Kathryn checked with him before carrying out the action.

'No!' It came out forcefully.

Kathryn looked her surprise. 'It's not a happy snap, Ric.'

'Print it for me and buy the copyright.'

'But...'

'If we don't buy it someone else will. As you said, it's prime fodder for gossip pages and I don't want it printed publicly,' he said decisively, acting on his gut instinct which was too strong for him to ignore.

'It's not our business to protect, Ric,' Kathryn reminded him, her eyes searching his for the reason.

He'd trained her to handle all the business that came into the Sydney office. She was in charge when he was elsewhere. He trusted her judgment. But this was personal. Deeply personal. And he couldn't let it go.

Funny after all these years and having had no contact with Lara Seymour since he'd been taken to Gundamurra...yet the sight of her, looking as though she was the victim of physical abuse by her husband, got to Ric.

And here was Kathryn, looking at him with eyes that questioned if he'd suddenly lost his marbles—green eyes, auburn hair cut in a short chic style, pretty face, trim figure always smartly dressed in a business suit—all in all a very attractive package, housing a brain that invariably displayed a quick intelligence. He liked her, wished her well in the marriage she was planning with her boyfriend who was a hot-shot dealer in a merchant bank.

In fact, he liked her very much and wasn't sure her fiancé was good enough for her. Yet he'd never *wanted* Kathryn himself, not how he'd wanted Lara Seymour.

To him she'd been the embodiment of perfect femininity; softly slender, idyllically proportioned, a wonderful flowing curtain of shiny blond hair, a face of features drawn with delicate distinction, eyes the sparkling blue of summer skies, a beautiful smile that was both shy and inviting, smooth unblemished skin that glowed with a sheen he had ached to touch, to stroke. He'd understood the phrase, a swanlike neck, in the way she moved her head. And she'd walked like a dancer, innately graceful.

Every aspect of her had given him intense riveting pleasure, yet she'd also embodied the mystique of the unattainable, compelling him to...but that was far in the past.

'Lara and I go way back, Kathryn,' he said quietly. 'She would hate having this exposed.'

'You...and Lara Chappel?' She looked astounded.

'Lara Seymour...'

'Is *she* why...' An embarrassed flush flooded up her neck and burned her cheeks. Her gaze was hastily switched to the computer screen. 'I'll do a print for you,' she muttered.

'Why what?' Ric pursued the point, curious to know what she was thinking.

A rueful glance. 'Not my business, Ric.'

'Say it anyway.'

A shrug that disowned any personal interest. 'People talk about you. Let's face it...you'd have to be one of the most eligible bachelors in the world. You could have your pick of beautiful women, yet...'

'Yet?'

She finally gave him a direct look. 'You never seem to have a serious relationship.'

His smile was wry. 'I lead a busy life, Kathryn.'

'Of course.' She nodded and busied herself producing a print of the photograph on glossy paper.

Ric pondered the question she'd raised.

Yes, it was easy enough to get dates with women he found attractive. Somehow the attraction never lasted very long. It usually ended up feeling false, with him becoming too conscious of how pleased the women were with what he could provide. They didn't *know* him. They just wanted the part of him that emanated the power of huge success and big money.

He'd certainly fulfilled his ambition of making it to the top. The world was more or less his oyster. He owned apartments in London and New York—prime properties—as well as in Sydney, with a magnificent harbour view. He also had classy cars in each city; a Jaguar in London, a Lamborghini in New York, a Ferrari here.

The Porsche he'd once stolen to impress Lara flitted through his mind. He could have bought one. Didn't want to. Why remind himself of frustration...defeat? Although he wasn't that boy anymore... was he?

Did anyone ever really escape the past?

Kathryn handed him the printed photograph and he stared down at it, feeling the past grab him back to that time and place when being with Lara Seymour had seemed more important than anything else. Somehow she'd been the fulfilment of all he'd craved for himself.

'Got an envelope for this?' he asked, knowing he was going to act on it.

Kathryn opened a desk drawer, gave him one.

'Print five more copies…' His instincts insisted on the precaution. 'Lock them in the safe. Then delete.'

She nodded, frowning over the unusual commands. 'What should I pay for the copyright?'

'I don't care.' He slid the photo into the envelope, sealed it, stood up. 'Negotiate the best price you can.' He threw her a look of reckless determination as he headed for the door. 'The bottom line is…I don't care how much it costs. Just do it.'

'Right!' she said, accepting the task without any further questions, though her eyes were full of them.

Ric didn't care. He could afford a stupid self-indulgence if that's what it was. It looked to him as though Lara was in a bad situation with Gary Chappel. The photo had been taken at the airport. Had she been attempting to run away from her husband?

Domestic abuse could occur in any household and all too often it was hidden through shame. And fear of more punishment. His own mother had been a victim of it—dying from ruptured kidneys when Ric was only a kid. He'd been too little to protect her, getting beatings for trying. At least his father had gone to jail for it, but Ric had never forgotten the fear of testifying against him in court.

If Lara was living in that kind of fear…

Ric found his hands clenching as he rode the elevator down to the basement car park. It wasn't his fight. He had no rights in this matter. Nevertheless, he couldn't ignore it. His heart burned with the need to act. And in his mind flared a wildly wanton exultation in having the power to do it—the power to do anything he chose to do.

He wasn't a street kid anymore.

He was a rich guy.

With class in spades.

And money to burn any way he liked.

In that respect, he could more than match Gary Chappel.

He was glad he'd dressed in his favourite Armani suit this morning, more for meeting Mitch Tyler for lunch in the city than for business. Barristers always dressed in suits and Mitch was a top-line barrister these days. He'd made it to where he wanted to be. Johnny Ellis had, as well, going platinum on quite a few of his country and western songs. Even after all these years since their time at Gundamurra, the three of them still connected when they were in the same place.

None of them had married.

As Ric got in his Ferrari, he wondered if Mitch and Johnny had the same problem with the women they dated, finding themselves more outside the relationship than in it after a while. The three of them probably understood each other more than any woman could. In fact, he might need Mitch to sort out Gary Chappel if that was what Lara wanted.

He drove out of the car park for the office building at Circular Quay and headed for the Eastern Suburbs. The envelope containing the photograph was on the passenger seat beside him—a major weapon in a war he could wage if Lara wanted to be free.

He knew where she lived. Not that he'd ever kept tabs on her. There'd been a splash of publicity when Gary Chappel had acquired the fifteen million dollar mansion on the harbour foreshore at Vaucluse—a photospread of Lara showing off the refurbishings they'd subsequently done.

The perfect hostess for her station in life, Ric had thought then. He hadn't imagined for one moment that her station in life might be miserable in private. It had seemed to him she was blessed with everything...and still unattainable as far as he was concerned. No point in manipulating a meeting with her. Leave the past in the past, he'd argued to himself. No good could come of it...only more frustration and defeat.

So why was he butting in now?

Because the picture he'd always had of her charmed life was askew.

What did he hope to achieve by intervention? Who did he think he was? Superguy to the rescue?

Well, it might turn out as a black joke on him, but Ric knew he wouldn't rest easy until he knew the truth behind that photograph.

Determination drove him to Vaucluse. Determination took him up to the massively colonnaded front porch and pressed the doorbell. Determination made him endure the long wait for the door to be opened—not by Lara, but by a middle-aged woman. The permed grey hair and royal blue button-through uniform dress instantly cast her as staff in Ric's mind. Probably the housekeeper.

'My name is Ric Donato. I've come to visit Mrs. Chappel,' he declared with even more determination.

'I'm sorry, Mr. Donato. Mrs. Chappel isn't receiving visitors today,' came the totally uncompromising statement. But it did reveal Lara was here.

'She'll see me,' he replied grimly, holding out the envelope. 'Please give this to Mrs. Chappel and tell her Ric Donato has come to discuss its contents with her. I'll wait for her reply.'

'Very well, sir.'

She took the envelope and closed the door in his face.

He waited.

In a way, it was blackmail. Lara would know it wasn't the only copy of the photograph. She would be afraid of what use he might make of it. Fear would open this door to him. Then he would be entering her life again.

For how long he didn't know.

He thought of it only as…something he couldn't turn away from.

CHAPTER TWO

LARA sat in the nursery, her feet automatically tipping the rocking chair back and forth in a rhythm that was supposed to soothe, although she knew nothing was going to lift the depression of being imprisoned in this life with Gary. She had to escape it. Had to. But how?

She stared bleakly at the empty cot, the empty pram, the empty everything she'd bought for the baby she didn't have. Stillborn. She wished she'd died with it. The ultimate escape. Probably the only one. Gary was too watchful of her to let her get away. Watchers everywhere.

All the same, she had to go before he made her pregnant again. She desperately hoped it hadn't happened last night. That would be unbearable. She'd managed to get

29

a packet of contraceptive pills from a pharmacy in Kings Cross, lying about leaving her prescription at home, promising to bring it in the next day. But she'd only been taking them for two weeks and wasn't sure they would work yet.

Having a child would trap her in this marriage forever. Impossible to flee. Gary would have the law after her in no time flat, getting custody. Everything within her cringed from the thought of leaving a child in his keeping. That couldn't be allowed to happen.

Marian Keith appeared at the doorway, holding a large white envelope. She was Gary's choice of housekeeper, a widow in her fifties who'd run into financial difficulties, having sons who needed helping through university and very grateful for the generous wage she earned here.

All the domestic staff were Gary's choices and they answered to him, not his wife. Yet occasionally Lara did catch a flash of sympathetic concern in the house-keeper's eyes. More than anyone else, Marian Keith saw what went on in this house. Not that she saw much. Gary was careful to keep his brand of tyranny private.

'Excuse me, Mrs. Chappel, there's a gentleman at the door…'

'You know I can't see visitors today, Mrs. Keith,' she said wearily, rocking on, her gaze drifting to the Walt Disney motifs printed on the wall. Snow White. Lara grimaced. She'd certainly eaten a poisoned apple when she'd married Gary Chappel. And there was no one to rescue her. No one.

'He was very insistent. A Mister Ric Donato…'

Shock slammed into Lara's heart. Her gaze jerked back to the housekeeper. 'Who?' she asked, not ready to accept what she'd heard.

'He said his name was Ric Donato.'

Unbelievable after all these years! Her mind spun back to the past. How many

times had she looked for him then, hoping
he'd turn up, wanting to be with him again,
not caring who he was or what he didn't
have. Ric Donato. Ricardo...

A lost dream.

One she'd buried as the years went by
with no sight of him, no contact with him.
Too late now. Impossible to let him see her
like this.

'He asked me to give this to you.'
Marian Keith came into the nursery, holding out the envelope. 'He's waiting at the
door. He said you'd want to discuss the
contents with him, Mrs. Chappel.'

Lara shook her head but she took the envelope and slit the flap open with her finger,
curious to see what was inside. She only
half removed the glossy sheet of paper, another more fearful shock hitting her at the
sight of the faces printed on it.

Her hand instinctively shoved the sheet
back in the envelope to keep it hidden. For
several moments her mind froze in sheer

terror of the consequences if the photograph was released to any form of the media.

'What should I tell him, Mrs. Chappel?'

Him... Ric Donato waiting at the door...prepared to discuss the contents...

She had no choice.

It was either see him or...

Her heart fluttered. Her chest was unbearably tight. She sucked in air and made the only decision that might save her from Gary's rage. 'Show Mister Donato out to the patio, Mrs. Keith. I'll see him there.'

Hesitation. Worry. 'Are you sure, Mrs. Chappel?'

Gary would find out she'd had a visitor. No escaping that. She would have to confess why. Dear God! There was no way out. But better to stop this from going public and take the punishment for causing the scene that had been so graphically captured by someone's camera.

'I'm sure, Mrs. Keith,' she said with far more confidence than she felt.

'Very well.' A nod of wary acquiescence and a brisk departure.

Lara couldn't bring herself to move. The envelope gripped in her hand felt like dynamite, the fuse already lit and nothing was going to stop it burning to a dreadful explosion. Even if she was able to block publication of the photo, Gary would hate anyone knowing about it and Ric Donato knew. She shrank from facing the knowledge in his eyes—dark eyes—like dark brown velvet, she had once thought, caressing her, making her feel...

She shuddered, automatically trying to shake off the memory. No point in it. Too much water under the bridge since then. She'd only been fifteen, Ric sixteen. It had been a wildly romantic fixation...a crazy dream...Romeo and Juliet...ending because it had never had a chance of surviving in the real world.

And surviving was what it was all about, Lara thought grimly.

She pushed herself out of the rocking chair. Mentally bracing herself for the inevitable meeting with Ric Donato, she made a quick trip to the downstairs powder room to check her appearance. Make-up almost hid the discolouration around her eye. Carefully drawn lipstick minimised the puffiness of her mouth. Her long blond hair, as always, was a smooth, shiny fall to her shoulders. Even around the house, Gary expected her to maintain an impeccable appearance.

She wore stone-coloured designer jeans and a long-sleeved brown and white striped shirt. The cuff covered the bruise around her wrist. Nothing showed except...she put on a pair of sunglasses—perfectly reasonable to wear them on the patio, considering the sun glare from the swimming pool.

Probably stupid pride, she mocked herself. Ric Donato was not about to be deceived. He hadn't come to be fobbed off, either, though why he had come...Lara took a deep breath in a desperate attempt to calm her inner agitation. He had to be faced, regardless of what motivation had brought him here.

She carried the envelope and its too revealing contents out to the patio, trying to quell the fear that was making mincemeat of her stomach. He was already there, standing under the sails that shaded the outdoors dining setting, gazing out at the sparkling blue waters of Sydney Harbour.

She was surprised to see him wearing a suit. The fabric and cut of it sharply reminded her of who Ric Donato was now— a man who could afford as many beautifully designed and tailored suits as he cared to own—a man who had the power to broadcast her private secrets to a gossip-hungry world. Over the years she'd read quite a few articles about him—prize-winning photo-journalist, moving into business with a network of photographic agencies around the world.

Yet she found herself staring at the black curly hair that was still worn long enough to dip over the back of his collar, remembering a much younger Ric Donato, remembering her fingers threading through the tight corkscrew curls...

One kiss.

That's all there'd been between them.

Just one kiss...

He turned abruptly as though suddenly sensing her presence. She couldn't look into his eyes—eyes that had to know where *she* was at now. Shame curled around her heart, squeezing unmercifully. How had her life come down to this hopeless prison of fear? It had been like a slippery slide...once on it, no way back.

'Hello, Lara.'

The soft deep voice caused her pulse to flutter. Still she couldn't bring herself to meet his gaze. She stared at his mouth—a full lower lip and an emphatically curved upper one. Sexy and sensual. An oddly compelling contrast to the strong chisel chin and the very masculine Roman nose.

She remembered how he'd kissed her... slowly, and oh so seductively, wooing the romantic soul she'd had then. If only she could go back to the past, make different choices, take different paths...

'Ric...' she forced herself to say with an acknowledging nod.

He gestured to the envelope in her hand. 'It was taken at the airport and sent to my Sydney Agency this morning. For sale to anyone interested in buying.'

'You haven't sold it on yet?' she pleaded in a frantic rush, unable to contain the flooding well of panic.

'No. And I won't, Lara,' he assured her. 'In fact, I've just called my executive assistant who told me she's secured the copyright.'

'I'll pay whatever the price was.'

He shook his head. 'It's irrelevant.'

Lara gestured haplessly. 'I don't understand. Why have you come if not to...'

'Make good on my investment?' His mouth quirked into an ironic grimace. 'Oddly enough, I came for you.'

'Me?' It came out as a squeak. Her throat was almost choked by a huge lump of chaotic emotion. She dragged her gaze up to his. Was it caring in his eyes? They burned with some indefinable purpose which certainly encompassed her, making her feel weirdly skittish.

'Take your sunglasses off, Lara. You don't have to hide from me.'

'I'm not...' She bit down on the lie, but to show her naked face...it was too humiliating. 'Can't you leave me with some pride, Ric?'

'This isn't about pride. It's about truth. Just between you and me,' he stated quietly, giving a promise she instinctively believed.

Besides, he had the photograph. Which he'd effectively quashed from publication. Didn't that prove he was keeping her situation under wraps?

With a defeated little shrug of resignation, she removed the glasses, revealing the swelling that reduced one of her eyes to a narrow, bloodshot slit. 'Black truth,' she said self-mockingly, fighting back the pricking of tears.

He nodded. 'I never told you my mother was a battered wife.'

Lara flinched at the brutal labelling of what he was seeing.

'She died of injuries my father inflicted when I was eight,' he went on, hammering home what could happen. 'As many times as I tried to protect her, to get in the way, to deflect his violence, I couldn't save her.'

'I'm sorry. I...' She shook her head, swallowing hard to hold back the threatening tears. 'No, you never told me,' she choked out, trying desperately to hang on to some dignity.

'But I can save *you*, Lara. If you want me to.'

'Oh, God!' Control was beyond her. She moved blindly to the closest chair, dragged it out from the table, collapsed onto it, and covered her face with her hands, propping her elbows on the table for some solid support as she wept over the impossible prospect of being *saved* from a husband who was never going to let her go.

She was horribly conscious of Ric Donato watching her, waiting. At least he didn't try to touch her or speak comforting words, which would have been unbearable. He remained on the other side of the table, as still as a statue, saying nothing, doing nothing, just giving her time to get herself together again. Which she did eventually, pride in terrible tatters, but as Ric had already said, this wasn't about pride.

'Thank you. But there's nothing you can do.' She lifted her head, letting him see that stark truth in her eyes. 'Except what you've done...with the photograph. I'm very grateful to you for...for blocking it, Ric.'

Still that dark burning in his eyes. 'At the airport...you were running from him?'

'I failed,' she admitted wretchedly. 'Everyone here...they all report to him. I can't go anywhere...without his knowing.'

'No support from your family, Lara?' he asked, frowning over her helplessness.

'My father suffered a stroke.' Her eyes mirrored the bleak irony of the situation. 'He's in one of the Chappel nursing homes. My mother doesn't want to hear anything against Gary. It's too...threatening...'

She didn't go on. Ric knew she was an only child. No siblings to turn to. As for friends, Gary chose them. She'd lost touch with the girlfriends who'd shared her modelling years.

'But you do want to leave him,' he pressed.

'Oh, yes.' She flashed him a derisive look. 'I'm not a masochist, Ric.'

'How much, Lara?' he challenged. 'How far would you be willing to go to have Gary Chappel out of your life?'

She shook her head defeatedly. 'It's not possible.'

'Yes, it is,' he said with such arrogant confidence it goaded her into a reply that snapped with a mountain of miserable frustration.

'Do you think I haven't tested what can and can't be done?'

'Would you spend a year on an Outback sheep station, away from everything you've known?'

The Outback? She'd never thought of that as an escape route. Had never been there. Knew no one there. Was completely ignorant of how people lived there. But they did *live*. And she'd be free of the fear—fear she knew all too intimately, ever constant.

'Yes,' she said, defying any other judgment he might make from the rich and privileged lifestyle that had always been her environment. Desperation bred desperate measures.

'Are you prepared to walk out with me now? No baggage. Just you, walking out and leaving all this behind.'

'With...you?'

Her mind whirled with this further shock. Ric Donato wasn't posing some theoretical situation. He was actually asking her...and she didn't know the man he was now. How could she agree to such drastic action when her only personal experience with him had become a teenager's romantic memory? That had been...eighteen years ago!

'I'm your safe passage, Lara,' he stated without so much as a flicker of an eyelash. 'I can get you to Gundamurra where you'll be protected from any possible pursuit by your husband. You'll have safe refuge there for the year it takes to get a divorce.'

Gundamurra…it sounded like the end of the earth…primitive…

'It's best if you choose quickly,' he coolly advised. 'If what you say is true, and everyone here reports to your husband, he may already know of my visit and be suspicious of it.'

'How can I trust you to do what you say you'll do?' she cried, the fear of consequences paralysing any decision-making process.

'I'm here. I'm offering. What have you got to lose by trusting me?'

'If you fail, it will be much, much worse.'

'I won't fail.'

'Gary said he'd have a man watching me. Watching the house. Watching where I go.'

'My car is parked at your front door. I have the resources to evade anyone who follows us.'

He spoke calmly, with an indomitable self-assurance that actually calmed the surge of panic that was screaming through her mind. In its place came a wild litany of hope. Could he do it? Could he really? Get her away to a safe place where Gary couldn't reach her?

An Outback sheep station.

Why not?

It had to be more *civilised* than living like this.

'It's your choice, Lara. It will be a different life, but at least a life where you can always breathe easy.'

She took a deep breath. 'This Gundamurra...it belongs to you?'

'No. But I have lived there. And you'll be made welcome. It's where you can get your head straight...if you want to.'

Freedom was all she could think about, but freedom might also have a price tag.

'If we do this...and succeed in getting there...I'll owe you big-time, Ric.'

His mouth softened into a whimsical little smile. 'This isn't a money issue.'

Money? She hadn't even thought of
money. Looking at the man he'd become—
powerful enough to challenge Gary, and
feeling his power reaching out and winding
around her...what did *he* want of her?

Was it only compassion for her situation
moving him to offer help? What if he was
like Gary, taking without caring what she
wanted? No, he couldn't be like that or he
wouldn't have spoken about his mother.
She was letting fear screw up her instincts.

'You can always pay me back whatever
you think you owe me after you get a divorce,' he dropped into her fretful silence.

'How will I manage a divorce if I'm...?'

'I know just the guy who can do that for
you. Don't worry about it, Lara. Mitch will
nail Gary Chappel to the wall so there'll be
no comeback from your *ex*-husband.'

She shook her head incredulously. This
was all happening so fast—promises being

held out that she desperately wanted to grab. 'Are you sure about this?'

'Absolutely.' His dark eyes glittered with more than determined purpose as he stepped forward and picked up the envelope she'd laid on the table. 'This photograph will be used to gain fair compensation for what you've suffered at Gary Chappel's hands.'

She stared at him, and the feeling that she'd had about Ric Donato as a teenager came flooding back—a driving, unstoppable force. But he had been stopped then...by the police for stealing a car.

No need for him to steal now. He had the wealth and power to make him unstoppable in any enterprise he chose to take on. With that recognition, hope grew in Lara's heart. Rightly or wrongly, she did trust him. Whatever the risk, his offer was worth taking. At least she should try it.

She scraped her chair back and stood up, adrenalin shooting new energy through her. 'I'll go and get ready.'

Decision made.

He nodded, acknowledging it, approving it. 'Bring nothing more than an ordinary handbag, Lara. Purse, driver's licence, what you'd normally carry on an outing. Okay?'

She was acutely aware of the sense in that instruction—nothing to suggest a final departure. 'I'll only be a couple of minutes, Ric. Wait here for me?'

'Yes. You can put your sunglasses on again.'

She did, then amazingly she found herself smiling at him, the heady promise of freedom lifting her heart. 'Thank you, Ric.'

He smiled back. 'I always wanted to be a white knight coming to the rescue of a fair damsel in distress. It feels good to be at your service, Lara. That's enough for me.'

It was a reassurance that she was safe with him.

He wouldn't demand anything of her.

Maybe fairy stories could happen in real life, Lara thought light-headedly, hurrying off to get a bag. Though she couldn't see Ric Donato as a white knight. More a dark prince.

But dark was good when it came to hiding.

If he could keep her safe from Gary, he would indeed be a prince.

CHAPTER THREE

THE minutes ticked by, every second ex-
cruciatingly long for Ric. He paced up and
down the patio, willing Lara not to change
her mind, not to give in to a burst of panic
over her decision. He kept checking his
watch. Time was critical. If someone had
reported his visit to Gary Chappel…if he
came home…a face-to-face confrontation
before they could get away might scuttle
everything.

Footsteps coming…

He moved to meet them, his whole body
wound tight with tension.

Lara…wearing a brown shoulder-bag
now and carrying a hat. 'Ready,' she declared, determination in her voice, and with
a slight lilt of excitement.

'Let's go,' he said, and there was not the slightest hesitation from her, much to Ric's relief.

The housekeeper was in the foyer. She looked anxiously at the two of them. 'Mrs. Chappel…?'

'I'm just going out for a while,' Lara answered, heading straight for the front door. 'We won't be long, Mrs. Keith.'

The housekeeper beat her to the door. 'Mrs. Chappel…' It was a plea for Lara to reconsider.

She knew what went on here, Ric thought, and didn't like it. He laid a hand on the housekeeper's shoulder, drawing her gaze to his. 'Don't worry. I'll look after her.'

She shook her head slightly but stepped back, letting them go without further protest.

'It's a conspicuous car, Ric,' Lara remarked fearfully as he loaded her into it.

'We won't be in it for long,' he assured her.

It was good to get behind the driver's wheel and fire the engine up. He had Lara in his custody now and nothing was going to stop him from flying her to Gundamurra. The temptation to leave in a burst of speed was strong, but the wiser course was to drive sedately, watching for the watchers.

He was no sooner out of the private driveway to Chappel's mansion, than a grey sedan, parked at the kerb on the street, started up and pulled out, quickly catching up to the Ferrari, sitting just behind it. A male driver, wearing sunglasses and a base-ball cap.

Ric had no intention of shaking him. That was better done when the follower least expected it. At the first red light, he used his car phone to contact his office at Circular Quay. It only took a few moments for Kathryn to come on line. He spoke to her as he drove on.

'Kathryn, I'm heading back to the office. I have Lara Chappel with me and I need your help. Clear your desk for the next couple of hours, grab your bag and car keys and be waiting for me in the basement car park. We should be there in about ten minutes. Okay?'

'I'll be standing by, Ric.'

'Tell your secretary you're off to a business meeting with a magazine editor and won't be back until after lunch.'

'Will do.'

'Thank you.'

'Who's Kathryn?' Lara instantly asked, her hands curling in her lap, clearly apprehensive about anyone knowing what they were doing.

'Kathryn Ledger. My executive assistant in the Sydney office. She has both my confidence and my trust.'

'Is she the one who bought the photo?'

'Yes.'

Lara took a deep breath. 'I take it we'll be switching cars.'

'Necessary. Don't jerk around in your seat to look. We're being followed by a guy in a grey sedan.'

The hands curled into white-knuckled fists.

Ric wondered just how many escape attempts had been thwarted. And punished. Irrelevant, he told himself. That was the past. He had to secure Lara's future.

At the next red light, he punched out the numbers for Bankstown Airport and made contact with the guy in charge of Johnny's Cessna.

'Ric Donato. I'll be taking Johnny's plane on a flight to Bourke. Can you get it on the tarmac with a flight plan lodged as soon as possible, please. I should be there in an hour or so.'

'I'll do my best, Mr. Donato. Want some refreshments on board?'

'Yes. There'll only be two of us.'

'No problem.'

He heard Lara take another deep breath. 'A private plane?' she asked tentatively.

He nodded. 'It belongs to a friend of mine. I have the authority to take it any time I want. Johnny's in the U.S. He won't be using it for a while.'

'You can fly?' An odd wonderment in her voice.

He threw her a confident smile. 'Don't worry. I have a pilot's licence and I've logged thousands of hours in the air.'

'Bourke...?'

'First stop. We'll get you some clothes before moving on.'

'I don't have much money with me. But I do have credit cards. If Gary doesn't...'

'No. No credit cards. You can be traced through using them. I'll supply the money. Consider it a loan.'

She didn't protest.

Ric was glad she had the presence of mind to take in the ramifications and not make any fuss over the plan he was still formulating. He was getting quite a buzz from it. Reminded him of his years in war zones when fast action and planning on the run were critical for survival. Lots of adrenalin rushes in those days. This was a different kind of battle but a battle nonetheless. Lara's life was at stake.

No doubt in his mind on that score. The black eye, the gut-wrenching weeping, the expressions of utter despair…that was more than enough to put Ric in fighting mode. The evidence of the guy following them sealed the truth of what Lara had told him. The Vaucluse mansion had been a prison and Gary Chappel deserved to lose his wife.

Whether the bastard had wrought irreparable damage on Lara, only time would tell. Ric was intent on giving her that time. Strange, after all these years, he still felt a strong tie to her. His first love. His only love, if it could be called that. More a fantasy, he told himself and Gary Chappel had more or less fitted into that fantasy. Except the truth of their marriage was very, very different to what he had imagined and Ric felt a hard cold fury toward the man who had brought Lara this low.

He glanced at her clenched hands, saw that she'd taken off her rings. A brave act, given her fear. Also a huge measure of her trust that he could, indeed, deliver what he'd promised. Which surely meant she did feel some positive connection to him. Perhaps a hangover from the past, remembering an *innocent* relationship between them.

Whatever…she had come with him and Ric was not about to abuse that trust in any shape or form. First and foremost she needed to feel safe. Then a swift, clean end to her marriage had to be accomplished. Which reminded him of his lunch date.

He called Mitch's chambers and left a message with his clerk, cancelling the luncheon and saying he'd contact him tonight.

'That's the barrister I spoke about,' he explained to Lara. 'Mitch will know how best to handle your divorce.'

'A barrister...' She glanced curiously at him. 'You have some very handy friends, Ric.'

Many friends, but only a few he could absolutely count on in this situation. 'Johnny and Mitch shared my time at Gundamurra,' he said matter-of-factly. 'And the man who owns the sheep station, Patrick Maguire, was like a father to us at a critical time in our lives. Each one of these men would do everything in their power to protect you, Lara.'

'Because you ask them to?'

He shook his head. 'Because they don't like people being hurt and not one of them would be intimidated by anything your husband could do.'

She heaved a ragged sigh. 'That might be a tall order.'

He threw her a devil-may-care grin. 'They're all tall men.'

It evoked a wry smile from her. 'You, too.' Then with a worried frown. 'I don't want Gary to cut you down. He's used to getting his own way, Ric. There will be…repercussions…from helping me.'

Amazing that she could be concerned for him and his friends when her own survival was on the line. 'There are times when a stand must be made, Lara,' he said quietly. 'And we are lesser people if we don't do it.'

There were so many injustices in the world. For years he had shown them through his camera, but the shots he had taken hadn't made any difference. They were simply a record of man's inhumanity to man. Maybe that was part of what was driving him today—the need to make a difference, if only to Lara's life.

He drove into the basement car park, using his office passcard to lift the barrier.

'Gary's guy can't follow us in here by car. We have time to make the swap. We'll both have to hunker down in Kathryn's car so he won't see us going out. You okay with that?'

'Yes.'

Kathryn was waiting.

The escape ran smoothly. No hitches anywhere along the line. By midafternoon they were in Bourke. Ric set up an account in a local bank, made Lara a signatory to it, withdrew several thousand dollars, gave the money to her and sent her shopping by herself. He also gave her the keys to the car he'd hired at the airport, now parked in Oxford Street. She could load her shopping bags in it whenever she wanted to.

'What will I need, Ric?' she asked anxiously. 'This is foreign territory for me. I want to fit in.'

Good positive attitude.

Ric was glad she had accepted the challenge of a year in the Outback, showing no traces of being a spoiled rich bitch who'd continually kick against the life. He wondered how she'd cope with the isolation, whether she'd welcome it or hate it. Only time would tell.

'Shorts, jeans, shirts, good walking shoes, sandals,' he rolled out. 'You'll need a warm jacket. A couple of sweaters. It can get cold at night out here. Think casual. Nothing too classy.' He shrugged. 'Look around you. See what the local people are wearing.'

Not that she'd be seeing any of them for the next couple of months. It was the end of February, still the wet season, and the road to Gundamurra would be washed out, impassable. The only way in and out was by plane. Even if Gary Chappel discovered where she was, he'd find it impossible to get to her. Patrick Maguire would see to that.

'You'll have to be quick, Lara,' he warned. 'We need to leave here by five

o'clock if we're to land at Gundamurra before sunset.'

'I'll be quick,' she promised, then suddenly grinned. 'No one's going to care what
I look like, are they?'

It was her first carefree expression. Ric
felt his own heart lift with pleasure. 'No
one will give a damn. You're not judged by
clothes in the Outback. It's the person you
are that counts, Lara.'

'The person...' She sobered, grimaced. 'I
lost the girl you once knew, Ric.'

He nodded. Impossible to go back.
They'd both grown beyond what they'd
been as teenagers. 'This is a chance to find
out who you are now,' he said, waving her
on to do her shopping. 'I'll meet you at the
car at five.'

He watched her quick jaunty walk up the
street, knew she was revelling in the first
taste of freedom. It was good, seeing her
without the fear, seeing *the difference*.
Reward enough for what he'd done.

The next step was to warn Patrick of their imminent arrival. He went to the post office to use the public telephone, wary of any record of the call being traced through his mobile. Luckily Patrick was in his home office not out in the paddocks.

'It's Ric,' he announced. 'I'm in Bourke. I'll be flying in to Gundamurra before sunset.'

'Great! I'll meet you at the airstrip.' Warm pleasure in his voice.

'Patrick, I'm bringing someone with me and I've promised she can be your house guest for a year.'

'A year?' Startled by the length of time.

Ric quickly explained the circumstances. Patrick listened, making no comment until everything had been told.

'This is your Lara, Ric?' he asked. 'The girl you stole the car for?'

His Lara. She'd never been *his*. Wasn't now. Yet... 'I had to rescue her, Patrick.

Will you keep her safe for me? She needs the time to put her marriage behind her.'

'It may not work out the way you want, son,' came the serious warning. 'No good her walking out of one prison into another, if that's how she feels about Gundamurra. But she's welcome here for as long as she's happy to stay.'

'That's all I ask.' The choice was Lara's. He couldn't—didn't want to—make her do anything against her will.

'Fair enough.'

'Thanks, Patrick.'

'I look forward to meeting her.'

It may not work out the way you want... Ric pondered those words as he strolled down the street to the Gecko Café where he could buy a coffee while he waited for Lara.

What did he want from this?

He knew what he didn't want—Lara being a battered wife.

But beyond setting her free from Gary Chappel...he wanted to see joy in her eyes...to recapture something of the girl that had once made every moment spent with her unbelievably special.

Magic.

Or was that a youthful dream, reaching for stars that were unreachable?

He shook his head, accepting Patrick's dictum that it may not work out how he wanted.

But it didn't kill the latent hope in his heart.

CHAPTER FOUR

RIC was leaning against the hood of the hire car, arms folded in a posture of relaxed patience. He'd left his suitcoat and tie in the plane. His shirt collar was open, sleeves rolled up his forearms.

Lara paused in her rush to the car. Seeing him like this, at a slight distance, she realised he had a more powerfully built physique than Gary. His arms were very muscular and his shoulders were still broad without any clever tailoring to make them seem so. He'd filled out quite a lot from the boy she remembered.

She'd never thought of a photographer as leading a hard physical life, but of course it could hardly have been a picnic in war zones. And if Ric had also worked on an Outback sheep station...

Though how had he come to Gundamurra in the first place?

An odd choice for a city boy.

He might be very wealthy now but he was certainly a different breed to the men she knew. That hadn't changed about Ric Donato. He was different and she still liked the difference. She'd never been afraid of it. It was attractive, exciting. But more than that, she knew instinctively he would never knowingly hurt her.

Was that because of seeing his mother hurt and hating it?

Even as a teenager he'd treated her as though she were some precious being to be handled with care, given every courtesy. Like a princess...

Well, she was little more than a beggar maid now, and what's more, she never wanted to be viewed as a princess again. She resumed walking, happy with the clothes she'd bought. No artifice about them. No stylish elegance. Now that she was free of Gary, she was going to be a person, not a clothes horse to be shown off as a man's possession.

Ric caught sight of her and snapped upright, ready to move. Action man, she thought with almost giddy joy, still amazed at how he had so personally effected her escape, even to flying her away in a private plane. Though they hadn't yet arrived at their final destination, she hastily reminded herself. Even so, she no longer cared where it was or what it was. Ric said it would be safe there and she believed him.

She believed him even more as they approached the landing strip at Gundamurra. The Australian expression—*out the back of Bourke*—took on real meaning as she gazed down at a vast flat landscape, seemingly endless inland plains, far from civilisation.

'How big is Gundamurra?' she asked.

'A hundred and sixty thousand acres,' came the mind-boggling reply. 'Patrick runs forty thousand sheep on it.'

Lara did the maths. 'You mean each sheep gets four acres to itself?'

He nodded. 'The feed can get very sparse out here.'

'How does Patrick get around such a huge property?'

'Plane, truck, horse, motorbike. Depends on what has to be done.'

'The buildings…it looks like a little village down there.'

'Homestead, overseer's house, jackeroos' quarters, the mess and the cook's house, shearing shed, maintenance sheds, station office, school. There's usually a staff of twelve. With families, there are about thirty people living on the station. You'll have ready company, though not what you're used to, and it is isolated. Mail comes and goes once a week. By plane.'

Like an island, sufficient unto itself, she thought, except it was surrounded by land, not water. 'What brought you to

Gundamurra, Ric?' How had he even heard of it?

He shrugged. 'When I was convicted of stealing the Porsche, the judge gave me a choice—time in a juvenile detention centre or working on an Outback station.'

So that was what had happened to him!

'Patrick had set up the work program as an alternative for kids who were prepared to give it a go,' Ric went on. 'At our first meeting he told us that Gundamurra meant ''Good day'' in the Aboriginal language, and he hoped we would always remember our arrival there as a good day in our lives.'

'And it was for you?'

'Very much so.'

She sighed in rueful memory of the night the police had caught them in the Porsche. Ric had cleared her of any complicity in the theft and her father...'My parents shuttled me straight off to boarding school and watched over me like a hawk after we were caught.'

He threw her a sardonic look. 'No more undesirable connections?'

'None without the *proper* connections,' she mocked right back. 'Every school vacation I was taken to a fashionable resort, away from any chance of meeting up with you. Or someone like you.'

'I did write to you from Gundamurra. Several letters.'

His voice was flat, non-judgmental, but she sensed the deep disappointment he would have felt at no reply. 'I didn't receive them, Ric.'

'No. I guessed not.'

'I'm sorry. My parents must have kept them from me. Destroyed them.'

'You were only fifteen, Lara,' he said wryly. 'I was no good for you then.'

'Yes, you were.' The words came out with such fierce emphasis, it drew a quizzical glance from him. 'I don't mean about the car,' she hastily explained, flustered by her own outburst. 'I really liked being with you, Ric.'

His mouth softened into a smile. His eyes softened, too...dark caressing velvet. 'I liked being with you, too,' he murmured, then switched his gaze back to the dirt airstrip where he had to land the plane.

She lapsed into silence, shaken by the strength of feeling that had so swiftly seized her. How could she *want* any man after her experience with Gary? Utter madness. Ric was her safe passage away from an abusive and destructive marriage. Being grateful to him, appreciating the fantastic effectiveness of his resources and the generosity behind his every act on her behalf...that was warranted. But *wanting* him...?

No. She was emotionally overwrought, off-balance. More likely she wanted to be cocooned by his protective strength. The clawing desire to feel safe was attached to him. But she had to detach it now. They were landing at Gundamurra. It was to be her safe haven, not Ric Donato. Somehow she had to regain at least some sense of who she was before she could even consider forming any relationship at all.

Gary's superficial charm had wooed her into marriage. Her parents' overwhelming approval of the match had also had its influence. Immense wealth had promised security and all the good things in life. But all those shining promises had been false and she had swallowed them. What did that say about her?

Time to take stock.

And this place certainly gave her the opportunity to do it.

Focus on Patrick Maguire, she sternly told herself. He was the constant around which her life on Gundamurra would revolve. A father figure to Ric. Maybe a benevolent father figure to her, too. She could do with a lot of benevolence.

He was waiting for them, a big man—huge—a giant of a man, standing by a four-wheel drive Land Rover as Ric taxied the plane back down the runway. 'Is he expecting me? Have you told him?' Lara suddenly thought to ask, the reality of actually being here rushing in on her, putting her nerves on edge.

'Yes. While you were shopping.' He gave her a reassuring smile. 'It's okay, Lara. You're welcome.'

She took a deep, calming breath. Ric had taken care of it, just as he'd taken care of everything else. She realised her mind had been in a fog of unreality all the way from Vaucluse to Bourke, not quite believing in what was happening, more letting it happen, taking the ride—any ride, as long as it was away from Gary.

Now she had to think, to act on her own behalf, to hopefully make a good impression on the man who was granting her space in his home until she could legally

free herself from her disastrous marriage—
a man whose protection she could count on,
Ric had said—protection given to a woman
he didn't even know. It was a gift she
hadn't done anything to deserve. Maybe
she could do some useful work here, at
least earn it.

Her mind was a whirl of wild anxiety
again by the time she and Ric emerged
from the plane, both of them carrying her
shopping bags. Did it look as though she'd
bought too much? Been too extravagant?
She was horribly conscious of the designer
outfit she was wearing, wishing she'd
thought to change into the more appropriate
clothes in the bags.

Patrick Maguire lifted the hatch at the
back of the Land Rover so they could load
the bags straight into the vehicle. 'Lara had
to leave with nothing. We bought this stuff
in Bourke,' Ric explained.

The old man nodded, making no comment. He had to be in his sixties or seven-

ties, though he wore his age well. The shock of white hair was still thick. There were deep lines in his face, particularly the crow's feet at the corners of his eyes, but there wasn't much loose skin. Strong bones, sharply delineated, though well-fleshed. Nothing scrawny or weak about this man of the land. His eyes were a steely grey and Lara could feel her insides quailing under their patient observation.

Ric closed the hatch door and made a formal introduction. 'Lara, this is Patrick Maguire. Patrick, Lara Chappel.'

'You're very welcome, Lara,' he said in a deep quiet voice, offering his hand.

'Thank you for…for taking me in.'

A slight frown drew his brows together and she realised her sunglasses made eye contact with her impossible. Worried that he might think her rude, she whipped them off.

'Sorry. I didn't mean to…' Hot embarrassment flooded up her neck and burned her cheeks as his eyes narrowed at the damage the glasses had hidden. She grimaced. 'I'm a bit of a mess. Please forgive the glasses.' She shoved them back on in an agony of self-consciousness.

He gently squeezed her hand, imparting a comforting warmth. 'Don't worry about it, Lara. You'll mend,' he said simply.

'I don't want to be a free-loader, Patrick,' she rushed out. 'I'll do whatever I can to earn my keep here.'

He nodded, giving her the sense he approved, though his reply was a measured one. 'Time for that when you find your feet. No need for you to feel anxious.'

'I just think...it would be good to be busy with something.'

Again he nodded. 'We'll talk about it after you've settled in. Okay?'

'Yes,' she quickly agreed, not wanting to seem demanding. This was such unfamiliar territory, she didn't know how to act.

Patrick released her hand, but he didn't move to usher her into his vehicle. He regarded them both with a distinct air of challenge, then stated, 'You should both know there have already been aggressive moves made to find you.'

Tension screamed through Lara. *Aggressive* meant…she could feel the blood starting to drain from her face, beads of sweat breaking out on her forehead as fear clamped its chilling grip on her heart.

'How do you know?' Ric asked.

'Mitch called earlier this afternoon, asking me if I'd heard from you. I hadn't and told him so.'

'Mitch…' Lara clutched at the name, trying to steady herself. 'The barrister Ric knows?'

Patrick nodded.

'Why would he call here?' Ric asked sharply.

'He wanted to make contact with you and thought you might be heading to

Gundamurra. He said no more at that point. After your call from Bourke, I realised there had to be trouble—maybe at your Sydney office—so I got in touch with Mitch and discussed the situation with him.'

'Oh God!' Lara groaned, turning anguished eyes to the man who'd put himself at risk for her. 'I did tell you. Gary won't let go, Ric. He's…he's…'

'I know what he is,' he flashed at her, his gaze returning to Patrick. 'What trouble?'

'No, you don't know,' she cried, plucking at his arm in frantic urgency. 'You haven't lived with him. I haven't told you. It won't stop, Ric. He'll go after you if he can't get at me. I shouldn't have let you do this. I shouldn't have…' She shook her head, realising she'd blinded herself to consequences for Ric in her need to believe escape was possible. 'I have to go back.'

'No!'

It was a violent negative, and she ached to give in to it, hide behind him as long as she could, but it wasn't fair. 'I don't want you to suffer because of me,' she shot back at him just as violently. 'It's all my fault for...for being such a fool to marry Gary in the first place.'

His dark eyes burned with the unshakeable purpose he'd shown before. 'I won't let you be his victim again, Lara.'

'You don't understand. He'll victimise you and your people. If he's already been to your office...'

'Kathryn must have gone to Mitch.' His gaze jerked back to Patrick. 'How was it handled?'

'Kathryn kept the situation contained. That will probably last until tomorrow. But to keep Lara safely hidden here, you'll have to leave, Ric, lay a trail elsewhere and let yourself be the target for pursuit.'

'No...no...' Lara protested, tortured by the trouble she was causing him.

Patrick kept on speaking, punching out the current problem. 'That will give Kathryn a legitimate line for her to take, to halt any further harassment at the Sydney office. Mitch will call tonight. He wants to speak to both of you. I'm telling you this now to give you time to prepare for what's coming.'

'It's not right,' she pleaded with Patrick, wanting him to see how wrong it was. 'I got myself into this.'

'Lara...' The steely grey eyes locked onto hers and while she saw compassion for her anguish, they also reflected the same steadfast purpose in Ric's. 'There is no going back,' he stated quietly. 'Ric has chosen his course. And I agree with it.'

'But...I didn't mean to...to...'

He smiled at her, and it was like a warm blanket of approval enfolding her, welcoming her into his world. 'You're a woman who cares for others. Which is right and good. But understand there are times when a man must act according to his sense of rightness. In the end, we all have to live with ourselves.'

Even the chaotic mess in her mind cleared enough to recognise the truth he had spoken.

It was an inarguable argument.

The decision was made.

Come what might, there was no going back.

CHAPTER FIVE

HAVING seen Lara to the guest suite Patrick had designated—there were four of them in the huge homestead which had been built to house the Maguire family and provide hospitality to any visitors—Ric left her to settle in and refresh herself before dinner.

Patrick had told her she was welcome to borrow any clothes from his daughters' rooms, if she found herself short of anything. They wouldn't mind. All three of them were pursuing careers elsewhere but they came home from time to time to check on Dad. Their mother had died from cancer a few years ago.

This information had been affably offered as they drove up from the airstrip, along with a quick, potted history of Gundamurra. Its obvious purpose had been to allay any fears Lara had about accepting a virtual stranger's hospitality. But there were other fears to be dealt with and Ric drove straight to the point when he joined Patrick in the sitting room.

'You were testing her.'

It was a flat statement, not open to question, and Ric searched the old man's eyes for the reasons why he had revealed what he had at the airstrip instead of waiting for a private man-to-man talk.

'It's been eighteen years. A youthful fixation might have impaired your judgment. I wanted to know if she was worth what bringing her here will cost you.'

'It's not a matter of price to me.'

'I know that, Ric. But you're not the only one involved in this now and I had to feel right about it.'

'Do you?'

'Yes. There was a chance she was just using you for her own ends. I remember your letters were never answered.'

'She never got them. Her parents...' He waved a dismissal of that issue. It was far in the past. It was the present and future that concerned him. 'Give me the details of what Mitch told you.'

'Apparently Gary Chappel stormed into your office during the lunch hour, demanding to know where you were. No one could tell him. He waited for Kathryn to return from her meeting. She told him you had a lunch date with an old friend and didn't know when or if you'd return to the office. He said your car was in the basement parking area. She said you had probably walked to the restaurant. He insisted on being given the name of the restaurant and she saw no harm in telling him. It got rid of him so she could contact Mitch for instructions.'

Ric nodded. 'That was my advice to her if Gary Chappel came to the office.'

'Mitch got the message during a court recess. He called her, got a rundown on what had happened, and immediately sent two of his people to escort Kathryn to the courtroom where he was arguing a case. When I last called, he was in his chambers and Kathryn was still with him.'

'Best I talk to him now then.'

Patrick nodded. 'Use my office.'

It worried Ric that Mitch had decided on protective measures for Kathryn. To his mind, the better course was for her to be innocently going about her work, as though nothing untoward had happened. Ric was not based in Sydney. He came. He went. He spent most of his time in London. To take Kathryn out of the office actually pin-pointed her as knowing more than she had admitted. It put her under a constant threat which was not what Ric had intended.

The moment he heard Mitch's voice on the other end of the line, he spilled out his concern. 'Mitch, have you still got Kathryn with you?'

'Yes. She's right here.'

'Why? I thought I'd left her covered. Won't this excessive caution make her a target?'

A pause.

Ric's nerves screwed up to piano-wire tightness.

'My gut feeling is that Gary Chappel will make her one,' came the measured reply. 'We're not dealing with a reasonable guy, Ric. I've seen the photograph. You did right to take Lara out. I'm behind this action one hundred percent.'

'I'm glad you agree. But Kathryn shouldn't be in danger. This isn't her fight.'

'Any way you look at it she's a link to you.'

His stomach churned. 'Can you keep her safe?'

'That's what I'm doing. But I need your cooperation, Ric. And Lara's. Especially Lara's. I take it she wants a divorce.'

'Yes.'

'I need to speak to her. Get the legal paperwork going as fast as possible. But first, it's best you get out of the area, Ric.'

'Patrick has already passed on that advice.'

'Good! Fly to Brisbane or Cairns tomorrow. Don't come back to Sydney.'

He'd have to arrange for Johnny's plane to be flown back to Bankstown Airport since he couldn't do it himself. Shouldn't be a problem.

'Catch the first available flight out,' Mitch went on. 'At the last minute, notify your office where you're going so it can be passed on to anyone who asks. It will distract attention from Kathryn who'll be taking a sick day tomorrow.'

'But when it's discovered I travelled alone…'

'It gives me time to put wheels in motion, Ric. Trust me. I'll handle this end of it.'

Ric took a deep breath to ease the tightness in his chest. 'I doubt legal paperwork will stop him, Mitch.'

'It stops an accusation of abduction. He can't get the law onside with him.'

'But it doesn't remove the threat he poses.'

'As soon as I've spoken to Lara, I intend to courier a copy of the photograph to Gary Chappel's father with a message to contact me.'

The tactic momentarily blew Ric's mind. 'Blackmail?'

'A manoeuvre,' Mitch corrected him. 'He'll come with his lawyer. We'll talk. Victor Chappel holds the reins of power in that family. If anyone can restrain his son, he's the man.'

'Counterthreats.' It might restore some balance to the situation, Ric thought hopefully.

'My reading is Victor Chappel will want to put a lid on this.'

'Will it work?'

'To a degree. My guess is it will move Gary into a covert operation. He'll be furious and his kind don't give up, Ric. You're going to have to watch your back. You took his wife from him.'

Ric frowned. Surely there would be an end to it one day. How long did fury last? He accepted having to go into exile, away from Lara, accepted he might be in danger for a while and he'd take steps to safeguard against it, but a lifelong vendetta? Only time would tell, he thought grimly. Meanwhile...

'What about Kathryn?'

'I think she'll be safe. I'll state the case very strongly to Victor Chappel that any further harassment of your office staff will have very public consequences.'

Ric breathed a huge sigh of relief.

'By this time tomorrow I should have things settled down at this end,' Mitch assured him.

'Thank you. I appreciate your help... more than I can say.'

Another pause. Mitch cleared his throat but his voice was uncharacteristically gruff when he spoke again. 'Patrick said...this is your Lara...from the old days.'

Ric closed his eyes, remembering how he'd talked about her in the bunkhouse at night. A boy's idyllic fantasy. Until the hard reality of getting no reply to his letters had straightened him up and forced him to face the truth that he could never be acceptable to her as he was.

Was he acceptable to her now? As more than just a white knight who had come to her rescue?

He shook his head. This wasn't the time to think about that.

'Yes. But that was a long time ago, Mitch,' he answered.

A heavy sigh. 'I would have told you about Gary Chappel if I'd known about her marrying him.'

'Told me what?'

'A guy like that doesn't change his attitude to women. It's not generally known but he has a history of abuse.'

Covered up, no doubt.

Ric felt his jaw clench. The power of wealth could hide a multitude of sins. But no power on earth was going to put Lara back in Gary Chappel's clutches. Over my dead body, Ric thought with a ferocity that tightened every muscle in his body to battle readiness.

'I'll do everything I can to contain him through legal means,' Mitch went on. 'You can count on that. I'm only sorry your Lara's caught in the middle of it.'

Ric managed to loosen his mouth enough to say, 'At least she's safe here.'

'Yes. And I'll keep Kathryn with me tonight.'

'What about her fiancé?

'He's in Melbourne on business.'

'Put Kathryn on for a moment, please Mitch.'

A pause while the receiver was handed over.

'I'm okay with all this, Ric,' she instantly assured him. 'And let me tell you I don't blame Lara Chappel for running. Her husband is one scary guy.'

'Promise me you'll do everything Mitch tells you, Kathryn. Take nothing for granted.'

'I will.'

'Good. And thank you again for your help. I'll be in contact once I reach L.A.'

'Take care.'

'You, too.'

She handed back to Mitch who immediately asked, 'Will Lara talk to me now?'

'Give me fifteen minutes. I'll call you back and put her on.'

Was Lara calm enough to give Mitch the information he needed? Time was clearly of the essence. Hoping she'd have the presence of mind to cooperate fully in telling Mitch all he needed to know, Ric strode around the veranda to the guest wing, hating the necessity to put her through this.

She'd already been through too much with her husband. Her fear of Chappel and what he could do was obviously based on experience that Ric could only guess at. *A history of abuse...* God only knew what that encompassed. Her white-faced panic over what Patrick had told them at the airstrip was sickening in itself. Was it even possible for her to think straight at this juncture?

He knocked on her door, knowing he had to persuade her to talk, yet inwardly recoiling from pressing her into it. He savagely wished he could have achieved her release from torment by himself, not involving others—just her and him—but that was as futile a dream as wishing for everything to be different. It wasn't. Never would be.

She opened the door and he just stood there, looking at her, unable to say a word, rendered speechless by a chaotic torrent of powerful emotions. *His Lara...*

She wore blue jeans and a blue and white checked shirt that still had the creases from its packaging. Despite the swollen and bruised eye and the years that had gone by, she looked fifteen—young, terribly vulnerable, and he desperately wanted to take her in his arms and promise that life would be good to her. She was safe with him. He would love her as she should be loved. Nothing to fear.

But she wasn't fifteen, and the years that separated them carried a weight he couldn't shift. Not yet. Perhaps not ever. One step at a time, he told himself.

'Mitch needs to talk to you now, Lara,' he stated bluntly, incapable of bringing any finesse to *this step*. Concentrating on action was the only way to hold his feelings at bay.

Her carriage stiffened, shoulders going back, chin up. 'I'm ready,' she said, clearly determined on doing whatever was asked of her to redress a situation that now endangered others.

He gestured for her to accompany him, intensely relieved that she had at least accepted they had moved beyond her going back to her husband. She stepped out of her room, closed the door and fell into step beside him.

'You've spoken to Mitch, Ric?' Tension in her voice.

'Yes.'

'Is Kathryn...safe?'

'Yes. She's with him.'

Her throat moved convulsively. She managed a ghost of a smile. 'I liked her. Is she...special to you?'

'As a business associate and a person, I value Kathryn very much but we've never had a private relationship. She's engaged to be married.' It suddenly seemed important to add, 'While I, on the other hand, have no romantic commitment to anyone.'

'Oh! I just...' She ducked her head, her long hair veiling the rush of heat into her cheeks. 'You seemed to have a good rapport with her.'

'I trained her to take the position she has in my business. It's given her a keen understanding of what I'm about.'

A nod. 'You're sure she's safe?'

The threat Gary posed was weighing heavily on her mind. Ric gave her a quick rundown of what Mitch had already done and intended to do.

'Victor doesn't want to know,' she said in bitter comment. 'Gary is his only son.'

'Believe me, Lara. Mitch is not going to allow Victor to turn a blind eye to what his son is.'

'I begged him for help. He wouldn't listen. He brushed off everything, saying it was between me and Gary to work out our...our *differences*.' There was a world of painful disillusionment in that last word. Helpless frustration, too.

'Tell Mitch,' Ric gently advised. 'It will be far more effective put in a legal context.'

Her hands started fretting at each other. 'I'll tell him, but…' An anguished glance at him. 'I'd rather speak to him alone.'

'I'll wait outside the office door. You can call me in if Mitch needs to speak to me again.'

Her breath shuddered out on a sigh of deep relief. 'Thank you.'

Shame. He knew it was an integral part of what she'd been through and nothing he said would take it away. Right now she couldn't bear him to hear the worst. Ric knew it would make no difference to what he felt about her but she wouldn't believe that yet. Nevertheless, she had to understand and appreciate the need for honesty.

They reached Patrick's office and he ushered her inside, saw her seated in the chair by the telephone. Before he picked up the receiver, he paused to emphasise the gravity of the situation. 'Lara, I know you're going to hate this, but you must give Mitch all the ammunition you can for him to go into battle. The photograph is good but if you can give him more...'

She nodded, her gaze evading his, the heat of humiliation still staining her cheeks. 'I won't hold back anything, Ric. I owe it...to all of you.'

'No.' He frowned at the responsibility she was loading onto herself. 'You owe it to yourself,' he said emphatically. 'The truth is what will set you free, Lara. And it's the best weapon you can give to Mitch to use on your behalf.'

She flashed him a look of flinty courage. 'I won't spare myself when so much is being done—being risked—for me. Call him, Ric. I'm ready.'

He got through to Mitch again and left Lara to it.

Outside the office, he paced up and down the veranda, needing to expend some of the violent energy stirred by thoughts of what she might have suffered at Gary Chappel's hands. His own hands kept clenching. It was just as well that Mitch was handling the Sydney end because Ric wasn't sure he could trust himself to act rationally if he was anywhere near the Chappels.

Best that he get himself right out of the way, and not just to separate himself from Lara and draw attention away from where she was.

She needed space from him, too.

Patrick would be better company for her. A father figure. Someone who didn't want any more from her than her own well-being. She'd grow confident again with Patrick, not feel ashamed. Able to be herself. No sense of having to measure up to a memory of what she was before Gary Chappel.

Yes. He could see he had to go. Yet it felt like hell, having to leave her. She didn't need him, he told himself. In fact, he might be harmful to the process of healing. No choice, anyway. No choice. He had to go.

The office door opened. He had no idea how much time had passed. Lara beckoned him. 'Mitch wants a further word with you, Ric.'

She looked pale, sick to her soul, but there was no trace of tears. He strode back into the office, picked up the receiver. 'Have you got what you need?' he rapped out, wanting this torment to be at an end for Lara.

'All except a fax with Lara's signature, appointing me her legal representative.'

'We'll do that now. Thanks for everything, Mitch.'

'Just leave it with me, Ric. Take care of yourself.'

'You, too.'

He switched on the office computer, then flicked an apologetic look at Lara. 'Almost done. I'll just type out what Mitch needs— authority to act on your behalf—you sign it and I'll fax it to him. Okay?'

She nodded.

It only took him a couple of minutes. Her hand was surprisingly steady as she wrote her name on the printed sheet. She stood with him, watching it go through the fax machine. Before Ric was aware of what he was doing, his arm was around her shoulders in a comforting hug. She didn't flinch from his touch. She actually leaned into him, much to Ric's relief...and a burst of private pleasure.

'It's over for you now,' he assured her.

She released a shuddering sign and rested her head wearily on his shoulder. 'It's the start of something else, Ric,' she said sadly. 'I'm worried for you, and everyone else this is touching.'

He rubbed his cheek over her hair, unable to resist the close contact, a surge of tenderness tempering the desire to feel a much more intimate bond with her. 'Don't worry on my account. I'm a survivor from way back.' Before temptation could get the better of him, he quickly added, 'We'd better join Patrick. No doubt he's kept dinner waiting for us.'

'Yes,' she agreed, lifting her head and giving him a wobbly smile. 'You're one of a kind, Ric Donato. Did you know that?'

He wanted to read more into her comment than there probably was. He'd rescued her. That made him special in her eyes. He disciplined himself into returning a reassuring smile. 'You'll find that Patrick is one of a kind, too. He'll be good for you, Lara. Be at ease with him.'

Her mouth tilted wryly. 'A pity I wasn't sent here with you all those years ago. A different life...'

'Don't look back. Look forward. Okay?'

'I'll try,' she promised.

He walked her to the door, casually dropping his arm from her shoulders as he opened it to usher her out. Giving comfort was one thing. Pressing it too far was something else. Yet as they walked around the veranda to the main body of the homestead, he reached out and took her hand, holding it as he had held it when they'd walked together a lifetime ago.

Her fingers fluttered for a moment, then settled, content to accept the feeling of friendly companionship. She'd been alone too long, Ric told himself. She needed to be connected to someone who cared about her.

He cared.

CHAPTER SIX

LARA couldn't sleep. Her mind kept churning over the events of the day. She knew whatever happened now was out of her control, not that she'd had control of anything much for a long time, but that had only affected her. She worried about Ric—what Gary might do to damage him and his business.

Almost unlimited wealth gave the Chappel family an insidious power. A corrupt power. And she didn't believe his father could stop his one and only son from using it. Victor didn't keep close tabs on Gary. He might think a caution from him—even a command from him—would be respected, but Lara knew better. Gary would agree up front, and do what he wanted behind Victor's back.

If she couldn't be got at, Ric would certainly be the object of his fury. Ric, who hadn't counted the cost when he'd rescued her. Ric, who'd held her hand tonight but would be gone tomorrow, a moving target for Gary to focus on. If something bad happened to him—her mind shied away from the all too possible outcomes—how could she bear it?

He'd been so good to her.

More than that, she felt...if Ric went out of her life again, there would be a terrible black hole that nothing could ever fill. There *was* a bond between them. She'd felt it growing again all day, strengthening, tunneling deep into her soul. It wasn't that she'd been so dependent on his initiatives. It was Ric himself. The way he was. The way he was to her—knowing intuitively what she needed, giving her his support, caring at a deeper level than she'd ever known before.

Her marriage had been completely barren of such caring, like a desert that bred only emotional nightmares, no oasis in sight. She was supposed to be at peace here, but how could she be with Ric going into danger because of her?

Sitting across from him at dinner tonight, watching him, listening to him talk to Patrick, she'd kept seeing the boy she'd known in the man, marvelling at how much he'd grown from that time, yet eerily staying the same—the expressions on his face, how he moved his hands, the cadence of his voice, his respectful manner toward her. Ric Donato...

He was certainly no disappointment to the memory she had of him. Far from it. If only...

No. It was stupid, futile to indulge in *if onlys*. She was here at Gundamurra, where Ric had found direction for his adult life. And it was an amazing place, not at all the primitive lifestyle she had imagined. There was even house staff to cook and clean.

The homestead was huge, constructed with four wings that enclosed a courtyard which, incredibly, had a fountain in the middle of its green lawn, not to mention garden beds in bloom and pepper trees to give shade.

A screened veranda ran around all four sides of the quadrangle and the rooms themselves were very civilised, indeed. Well kept antiques graced the sitting and dining rooms, and even in this guest suite the chest of drawers and dresser were beautifully polished cedar pieces, and the patchwork quilt on the queen size bed was a work of considerable artistry.

It all projected a sense of solid old-time values that would outlast anything a more sophisticated world would declare *in* as *must haves* if one was to be up to date with modern fashion. The refurbishing of the Vaucluse mansion had been an exercise in creating the *right* image—all for show, nothing to do with setting up a home that actually felt like a home.

Cold rooms. Almost clinically perfect, but no personality in them. How could they be anything else when they were the work of interior decorators who were never going to live there? And, of course, Gary had been the one they'd consulted with, not her. She'd very quickly learnt not to change anything, not to offer any input. Best to smile and agree to everything.

But that was over now.

Look forward, not back, Ric had told her.

Except looking forward encompassed Ric's departure tomorrow and she was frightened of what that might lead to. If she was safe here, why couldn't he stay, too? Why did he have to put himself at risk? Or was that hopelessly selfish thinking, wanting him to be with her?

Her life could be put in limbo at Gundamurra, but Ric had an international business to run, other people depending on him. It would be totally unfair of her to beg him to stay. He'd done more than enough for her. Yet if she lost him again...

Footsteps were coming along the veranda outside her suite. It had to be Ric. He'd be sleeping in this wing, too. After dinner, Patrick had suggested she retire, noting how tired and strained she looked. True enough, but she'd guessed the two men had much to say to each other in private so she'd left them to it, though she would have preferred their company to her own.

She did feel washed out physically. Mentally and emotionally, too. But her mind couldn't be shut down. Maybe it would some time in the night...and if she was still asleep when Ric left in the morning...

Ric was going by now...

She hurtled out of bed and raced to the door which opened onto the veranda, her heart pumping with an urgency that couldn't be denied. The footsteps had already gone past and when she stepped out she could only see the back of him walking away from her, a shadowy figure in the darkness—too shadowy when she desperately wanted the reality of him.

'Ric!'

He stopped. It seemed an aeon before he turned, making her wonder if she'd mistaken someone else for him. Riven with doubts, she shrank back against the doorway, acutely conscious of not having paused to put on the dressing gown she'd bought. While the cotton pyjamas were a decent enough covering, they were no armour for confronting a man in the middle of the night.

Her rioting nerves were somewhat soothed as she caught the silhouette of his profile. It *was* Ric, looking back at her, half turning, holding his distance but at least acknowledging her call.

'Do you need something, Lara?' he asked quietly.

You. I need you.

The words pounded through her mind.

She couldn't say them.

They asked too much.

She simply stood there staring at him, barely able to contain the turbulent yearning that pressed her to run to him, fling her arms around him, never let him go. Maybe the power of it tugged at him. After a pause that screamed for answers he slowly retraced his steps toward her, coming to a halt an arm's length away, looking at her with what felt like a fierce concentration of energy.

'Are you having trouble sleeping? Would you like me to…?'

'No. I mean yes…I can't sleep,' she gabbled.

'I doubt Patrick keeps sleeping pills in the medical kit. Perhaps a drink of hot chocolate…'

'No...no...I just...' She took a deep breath, trying to pull herself together, be reasonable.

'Are you frightened, Lara?' he asked softly.

The words burst from her before she could stop them. 'Will you hold me? For just this one night, Ric. Will you hold me?'

The raw plea *was* a cry of fear—fear that she might never have any more of him than this—fear that Gary might take Ric from her, too, along with everything else he had taken from her—fear that her life would always be dominated by the loss of what should have been.

She saw Ric's chest expand as he sucked in a deep breath. Her senses registered a harnessing of strength but she was too chaotically needful to discern if it was meant for giving or rejecting. She could only wait and hope, every nerve in her body tense with a desperation that craved the caring he had shown her.

'Lara...' Was that the sound of longing, too, borne on his gruff whisper? But he didn't move. He didn't reach out to her.

'Please...?' she begged, fighting the restraint her instincts were picking up. She plunged on with wild argument, her hands fluttering, reaching out to him in frantic appeal. 'It mightn't be sensible. It might be mad. But you'll be gone tomorrow and I...'

Ric couldn't stop himself. His feet responded before his brain even attempted to countermand them, stepping forward of their own accord, and his arms scooped her into his embrace, precluding any other course of action. Her soft, slender body sagged against his and her arms lifted to wind around his neck, locking him into holding her.

It was the strangeness of being in an alien environment, he told himself, feeling alone and frightened of what the future held for her. She needed comfort, reassurance.

He was the only familiar person for her to hang on to. She wasn't asking for any sign of the flood of passionate possessiveness that was surging through him, dragging at the vestiges of reason he was clinging to. He had no right to claim her as his. *No right...*

She nestled her face against his bare throat. He hoped she couldn't feel the wild beating of his pulse. Her breasts were pressed against his chest. He had to fight off the temptation to slide his arms down and haul her closer, fitting her stomach and thighs to his, craving the feel of her entire femininity, the essence of what had always made her desirable to him.

He felt his own body stirring and spoke quickly to distract himself from the sexual arousal she couldn't want from him. 'You will be safe here, Lara. I promise you,' he said emphatically.

'I wish you could stay with me.'

The yearning murmur struck chords in him that threatened to overwhelm all common sense. The warmth of her mouth moving against his skin shot an insidiously exciting heat through his bloodstream.

'I'll be back,' he assured her, his voice terse with the strain of having to exert intense control. 'It's just a matter of time.'

'Time...' She heaved a sigh that played havoc with his good intentions. 'So much of it has already gone by, Ric. Years... years of missing you,' she whispered.

He sucked in a quick breath, desperate for a shot of oxygen to clear his brain of the wild exultation her words had triggered. She couldn't mean what she was saying. Surely she'd had a good life before she'd married Gary Chappel...a successful model, feted and admired...

'I don't want to lose you again,' she went on, her voice a throb of fierce passion, whipping up the desire that had to be contained.

'You don't have to worry. It will all work out,' he assured her, then driven to take some diversionary action, he moved her to his side, intent on walking her back into her room. 'Come on. When you wake up tomorrow, you'll feel like a free woman.'

He got her inside, meaning to tuck her into bed, sit with her for a while, but she stopped before they reached the bed, turning to him with a frantic rush of words. 'What if he takes you, too? He's taken so much from me. If he gets to you, Ric…do you think I could ever feel free?'

Was it simply fear for him, driving this violent emotion? He rested his hands on her shoulders, gently kneading the tense muscles there. 'Lara…it's best that I go.'

He saw the glitter of tears in her eyes. 'I can't bear it,' she cried and threw herself at him, wrapping her arms around his waist.

She was so close, it felt as though her

heart was thumping against his. He couldn't think, didn't want to think. His hands traced the curve of her spine, the pit of her back, touching all he could allow himself to touch. His face buried itself in her silky hair, rubbing, kissing, breathing it in.

This was Lara…not a figment of his imagination but flesh and blood reality, setting him on fire for what he had missed over the years. He filled his senses with her, hoarding it all in his memory, craving more yet afraid of taking more than he should in this time and place.

As it was, there was no quelling the erection that telegraphed the desire he'd tried to hide. He expected her to ease away from him, expected a rush of mutual embarrassment that he'd somehow have to handle with some finesse, excusing it on some specious grounds that he'd have to bend his mind to. Soon…when she shifted…when it didn't feel right to her…

But she hung on so hard, it seemed she'd burrow right into him if she could, as though his warmth and strength was the elixir of life to her. She had to know he was reacting to it, reacting as a man, not as a chivalrous white knight whose only wish was to help. He was a man, burning to take her as his woman.

Her head lifted.

He didn't want to look her in the eye, didn't want her to see…

'Kiss me, Ric.'

His gaze sliced to hers, disbelief and rampant desire in instant battle. Had he misheard the soft whisper that echoed the deep ache in him?

'Please?' she pressed, her face tilted to his in open invitation. 'Kiss me like you did when we knew nothing else. Wipe out all the rest. Please?'

The memory came sharp and clear, banishing any resistance he might have mustered. His head bent to hers, the compulsion to recapture what had been lost directing the kiss he gave her, a gentle grazing of his lips over hers, a soft, slow tasting that was strangely bittersweet because he was so acutely aware of her vulnerability, the damage that had been done to her.

Innocence was forever gone. He couldn't bring it back, yet her tremulous, tentative response, her compliance to his initiatives, the hint of eagerness to explore more... eighteen years fell away and the love he'd wanted to show her at sixteen poured into his kiss.

He didn't intend it to change into something else. Did she spur it on? Or was it the years of sexual experience urging him to take her on a deeper journey where passion flared and hungered for more and more satisfaction? One kiss wasn't enough. One kiss incited an exhilarating ardour for more. And more.

She was travelling with him, her whole body telling him this was what she wanted too, her mouth barely leaving his for breath, intensely giving, her hands raking down his back, pulling him into her, her stomach rubbing against his erection as though wantonly stroking it, savouring his desire for her, revelling in it.

A crazy triumph was bubbling through his mind. Lara *was* his. She was giving herself to him. The sheer power of their need for each other made it right...didn't it? It had to. His body was screaming for the ultimate satisfaction of bonding intimately with hers. He moved them toward the bed, his hands sliding under the elastic waistband of her pyjama pants, getting ready to...

A bolt of sanity hit him, shocking him into an abrupt halt.

'Don't stop, Ric. Please?'

The feverish pleading seduced all reason for a moment...but he'd pledged her safety and to keep on going without...

'Lara...' Anguish writhed through him. 'I don't have any protection with me. We must stop.'

CHAPTER SEVEN

PROTECTION?

Bubbles of hysteria fizzed through Lara's brain. There'd been no protection from Gary's loveless demands on her, and Ric was stopping because he was worried about getting her pregnant? If it was going to happen, it would have happened last night so what difference did it make?

The only difference—the huge difference—was she wanted this with Ric... wanted it with every atom of her being. This was how it should be...what she was feeling with him...and if she didn't have it now...

'It's all right. I'm on the pill,' she rushed out in reckless disregard for whether it would provide effective protection or not.

123

Why should she let Ric care about it when Gary…

No, she wouldn't let herself think about last night.

This was tonight.

And she wanted her mind filled with Ric and the incredibly wonderful sensations of being loved instead of brutally used. She wanted to feel *his* hands moving over her again, caring hands, exciting sensual hands that knew how to caress, not hurt. And his mouth, kissing her with the heat of real passion—passion she could happily glory in because it felt so marvellous.

'I don't want to hurt you,' he said, his voice edged with strain. 'I'm sorry. I wasn't thinking…'

'You won't hurt me.' She believed that implicitly. It wasn't in him to hurt.

He shook his head, frowning more concern. 'If you have other bruising, Lara…'

'No. I stopped fighting,' she cried, desperate for his understanding. 'It was better not to fight. Oh God!' Her hands lifted in a desperate plea. 'Don't remind me. Don't let him come between us. Not between *us*. He always wins.'

But not this time. A feverish determination overrode the panic welling up. She had to stop Ric's retreat from her. Gary was not going to win tonight. Not tonight.

Her hands were trembling as she reached for the buttons on Ric's shirt, wildly intent on forcing another start to what had to be finished, her fingers fumbling but acting fast and obsessively focused. His tautly muscled chest rose and fell as she dragged the opening apart, then stood staring at what she'd laid bare, scarcely believing she'd been so bold.

He wasn't smooth-skinned like Gary. A nest of tight black curls arced between his nipples and arrowed down to the waistband of his trousers. Somehow it made him more elementally male—very different—not polished and sophisticated. A real man. A true man. The kind of man who protected his woman.

Except she didn't want to be protected from knowing all of Ric Donato. Did he understand now? Stunned by what she had already done, Lara was in a weird state of paralysis, still hanging on to the edges of Ric's shirt. It was an enormous relief when his hands covered hers, loosening their grip, carrying them down to her sides.

But did this mean he was about to step away?

Leave her?

She looked up in agonised protest. His face looked hard, tightly drawn, and his eyes glittered, as though ablaze from some inner fire.

'Are you sure about this, Lara?'

Firm command in his voice. Unshakable control.

He was giving her the choice, insisting she have it. Not like Gary. Not one bit like Gary. A leaden weight lifted from her heart. The tight ache in her chest eased. This wasn't rejection. It was a gift being offered and a wave of intense relief washed over the frantic worry that he saw something wrong in her...too wrong for him to get more deeply involved.

'I *am* sure,' she cried. No pause to reconsider. 'I want you, Ric. I need you.'

Doubts raged through his mind but denying her at this point was impossible. Need, desire, whatever it was for her...he could only hope it was right to go on, that it wouldn't turn out to be terribly wrong afterward.

He lifted her hands, pressed their palms against his bared chest, felt his heart hammering as though it wanted to break free of its cage of flesh and be held by her. He fiercely cautioned himself to move slowly, give her the chance to call a halt. The violence of his own need had to be contained, channelled into giving Lara as much pleasure as he could—pleasure to blot out whatever she had endured at her husband's hands.

He had to leave her with a good memory—one that gave her hope for the future—one that taught her all men were not the same as the bastard she'd married. She was asking this of him tonight, not somewhere down the track. Ric was acutely aware of the risk that he might simply be a turning point for her, yet if it was more than that…if she had missed him down the years…

It could be right.

He wanted it to be right.

He needed it to be right.

Without any haste, he undid the buttons on her pyjama top and drew it slowly over her shoulders, down her upper arms. She slid her hands down his chest, dropping them to let the garment fall to the floor. She stood absolutely motionless, tense with anticipation—or was it fear?—waiting to see how he would touch her.

Ric discarded his own shirt, making them equal, sharing the same amount of nakedness, the same vulnerability. Yet it wasn't the same because he was a man with a man's superior strength and that was all too obvious. He took her hands again, his fingers gently stroking reassurance, intertwining with hers. He felt her relaxing, looking at him with trust.

It was all right.

She wasn't afraid of him.

He caressed her arms with a feather-light touch, loving the satin smoothness of her skin. It gleamed with a pearly sheen in the darkness which no longer seemed so dark. He could see her quite clearly, the feminine slope of her shoulders, her long graceful neck, the proud thrust of her breasts.

He traced the curves of them, learning their shape, revelling in the freedom to do

it, filling his hands with her beautiful soft-
ness, his thumbs tenderly grazing over her
nipples, arousing an alluring tautness.

Her breathing quickened but she didn't
stop him. In fact, she reached out, tentatively touching him, surprising him further
with a husky plea. 'I want to see you, too,
Ric. Know all of you.'

He was happy to oblige, removing the
rest of his clothes, then her pyjama pants,
gliding his fingertips back over her calves,
behind her knees, up her thighs, feeling her
quiver under his touch but not flinching
away from it. He cupped the more volup-
tuous curves of her bottom and drew her
into full body contact with him.

She came willingly, once more winding
her arms around his neck, lifting her face
to be kissed, and as he rained tender kisses
around her temples, on her cheeks, nose,
mouth, she swayed against him in a kind of
shy, experimental manner, not deliberately
sensual yet it was incredibly tantalising,

stoking the desire he was battling to contain.

His passion for her flared again, whipping into urgency. It was difficult to think beyond the need surging through him. Yet he had to know she was ready, too, not just exploring how it felt with him. He moved them to the bed, lifting her onto it, sliding down beside her to avoid the most tempting contact.

He kissed her breasts as he slid his hand down to the apex of her thighs, stroking to see if she would open to him. No resistance. No reluctance. She welcomed his touch with a moist heat that drove his excitement higher.

Her fingers were scrabbling through his hair, tugging, pressing, and he moved to her erratic rhythm, drawing her nipples deep into his mouth, applying suction, releasing it. Her back arched up to him. She was breathing in quick little gasps.

He shifted his body, trailing kisses down her stomach, positioning himself between her legs, moving his mouth to the centre of her sexuality, wanting to deliver maximum excitement, using all the sexual expertise he had learnt over the years, needing to show her what she should feel, gently pushing her to the pinnacle of ultimate pleasure.

She moaned, arched higher, her inner muscles convulsing against the caress of his fingers as he worked what he knew was blissful magic—enthralling, ecstatic ripples of sensation that seized every bit of consciousness, honing it toward the only possible end, the climax of all a man and woman could feel together.

'Enough…enough…please…I want *you,* Ric.'

Her hands plucking at his shoulders, needing to drag him up, have him inside her. He didn't have to think anymore, didn't have to hold back. He surged forward, entering her with a swift plunge as he covered her wildly arcing body, exulting in her moan of satisfaction as she felt the full power of himself going deep, answering the sweet ache, releasing the built-up tension.

Having reached the innermost heart of her, he covered her mouth with his, kissing gently, asking the question, needing her response to be positive because he'd gone past the point of no return. Her tongue tangled with his in a slow wondrous dance, almost as though she was awed by the connection.

It was enough.

More than enough.

It was incredibly exhilarating feeling her body moving to match the rhythm of his, her legs goading him faster, giving herself entirely to the intensity of their union. To Ric it was the most powerfully moving act of his life—joining so intimately with Lara, feeling her welcoming him, wanting this with all her being, just as he did.

Aware she had already climaxed, Ric still held off his own as long as he could, revelling in the sensation of Lara giving herself to him with a totality that fulfilled every dream he'd ever had about her—a memory to cherish while he had to be away from her. When the tension inside him finally burst into release, Ric was riding the high of his life, and once it was over and he gathered Lara into his arms, holding her to his heart, he knew what happiness was.

Having this woman.

Holding her.

Loving her.

And feeling her love for him.

CHAPTER EIGHT

A LOUD droning sound penetrated Lara's slumber and snapped her awake.

The plane!

Ric...gone from beside her...flying away!

She leapt out of bed, realised she was naked, grabbed the dressing-gown from the chair in front of the dresser, thrust her arms into its sleeves as fast as she could, and wrapped it around her as she rushed to the door that led onto the veranda.

Too late to say goodbye. The plane would already be in the sky now. But she wanted to see it, if only to feel Ric was safe in the pilot's seat and the flight was going smoothly. She just caught a glimpse of it passing overhead. Then it was gone beyond the roof of the homestead and all she could do was listen until the sound of it was gone, too.

'Safe journey, Ric,' she murmured, willing him to get beyond Gary's reach as fast as possible and remain safe.

A sad deflation hit her as she walked back into her room. It was impossible to project how long it would be before she saw Ric again. *If* she saw him again. Her heart cringed at that thought. He'd said he would come back. She had to believe he would because she was in a helpless position to change any of the circumstances for him or anyone else. Everything to do with Gary was out of her hands.

Much stronger hands than hers were dealing with it now, she told herself, but she was still frightened for Ric, despite all his reassurances. He'd been so good to her, good in every way, and she was fiercely glad she had the memory of how it had been with him—the loving of a man who knew how to love, making her feel beautiful and precious, intensely cherished and cared for.

Her gaze fell on the indentation left by his head on the pillow beside hers. She crawled across the bed and buried her face in it, wanting to breathe in whatever scent of him was left behind. She closed her eyes and concentrated on remembering all the pleasure he'd given her from the lightest tingling touch to the final crescendo of incredible sensation that had tipped her into a sea of ecstasy.

How long had she floated there in blissful contentment while Ric had simply held her? It had seemed like time itself had stopped and they were in a world of their own, complete unto itself. She remembered listening to his heartbeat, stroking *his* body with a sense of awe, wanting him to feel how he had made her feel—incredibly special—because he was.

She wished she'd told him that.

Somehow last night the feeling of sharing something totally overwhelming had been so strong, so deep, words had seemed trivial, useless for expressing what had gone beyond anything that could be described. The silent, physical communication had seemed more right—just being together.

Had Ric understood?

Should she have said something?

Thank you were the only words she had spoken. And his mouth and eyes had smiled. No other reply. None necessary. He'd given what she'd asked of him. He was happy she was satisfied. And she didn't have to be told the pleasure had been mutual.

So it had all been good.

No regrets on either side.

She sighed and rolled over, knowing she had to face this day—without Ric—and take whatever steps she could toward making a different life for herself.

I won't let you down, Ric, she silently promised. *No matter what happens, I will become a better, stronger person because of what you've done for me.*

Having made this resolution, Lara got up and moved purposefully to the ensuite bathroom. A clean start, she thought. As clean as she could make it. No looking back.

Half an hour later she was showered, dressed, hair brushed, a touch of make-up applied to diminish the discolouration around her eye which was much less swollen this morning, rooms tidied and bed made. She walked around the veranda to the main body of the house and found her way to the kitchen, a huge utility room where three women were busy rolling out pastry on marble slabs and the smell of freshly baked bread instantly whetted her appetite.

The women—all of them part Aboriginal—stopped chatting when they saw her. Lara smiled and said, 'Hi!' but they just stared back until Evelyn, the housekeeper, whom she'd met last night, took charge of introductions.

'You're looking a lot better this morning, Miss Lara,' she said approvingly. 'These are my helpers, Brenda and Gail.'

'We're making pies for the men,' Brenda declared, a young curly-haired woman, probably in her twenties, merry brown eyes.

'Lamb and potato,' Gail added. She was about the same age, darker skinned, rather wildly dyed red hair, and a grin that beamed an attitude of finding fun in everything. 'I told Mister Ric he was missing out by going so early.'

'He had a good breakfast before he flew off,' Evelyn stated firmly as though Lara needed to be assured of it. She was a big woman, her salt and pepper hair marking her as middle-aged but wearing her years well, her plump good-humoured face relatively unlined. 'Now what about you, Miss Lara? There's still some pancake mix or I could cook you some eggs. What would you like?'

'We've got plenty of eggs from the chicken run,' Brenda added as she saw Lara hesitate.

All three faces looked at her, beaming an eagerness to please. It assured Lara they were happy to welcome her amongst them and she relaxed, warming to the cosy atmosphere in the kitchen. 'What I'd really like is a couple of slices of your fresh bread. It smells wonderful.'

They laughed, inviting her to sit at the big kitchen table while they worked around her. Two thick slabs of bread were cut. A tub of butter and jars of honey, vegemite and fruit conserve were laid out for her use. A pot of tea—her preference—was quickly produced.

Lara enjoyed her breakfast and the conversation which revolved around good-humoured answers to her questions about Gundamurra. She wasn't asked any questions about herself. It seemed her presence was simply accepted and the women were happily intent on drawing her into their community.

Their husbands worked on the station, carrying out maintenance and moving the sheep from paddock to paddock. Their children went to school here, lessons supervised by the overseer's wife and directed by radio from The School Of The Air. While the Paroo River ran through the property, most of the water used came from bores. There were beef cattle, as well as sheep, though they were more a sideline to the main business which revolved around stud rams and first class wool.

'Where is Mister Maguire this morning?' she asked, wondering when she would meet her host again.

'In his office,' Evelyn replied. 'I am to show you through the homestead before taking you to him. Make sure you know where everything is.'

'Thank you.' She smiled. 'I must say every room I've been in is beautifully kept, Evelyn.'

The housekeeper beamed with pleasure. 'Mrs. Maguire trained me herself,' she stated proudly. 'I am training the girls, just as she told me.'

'Well, you do a great job, Evelyn.' It was on the tip of Lara's tongue to offer her own help, but decided it was best if she speak to Patrick first in case she'd be treading on the toes of the domestic staff, butting in where she shouldn't be.

The tour of the homestead gave her a broader appreciation of how life was lived here. Adjacent to the large laundry was a mud room, stocked with raincoats, akubra hats and boots, clearly the first and last stop for those working outside. A bathroom completed the facilities for cleaning up before moving into the main body of the house.

'Have you had much rain?' Lara inquired.

'Many storms this time of year. Which
is good. We need the rain. It's hard to keep
everything going in times of drought.'

Lara had seen television coverage on the
devastation of long periods of drought in
pastoral Australia. It had evoked both horror and sympathy but the visuals had been
so far removed from her own life, the feelings had been only momentary. It would
undoubtedly have more impact on her now
she had entered this different world.

Though it was certainly not without
many civilised amenities. The billiard room
was also a library and music room, open
for use to anyone on the station. Walls of
shelves contained an amazing selection of
fiction and non-fiction books, videos and
CDs. A generator supplied electricity and a
satellite disk gave them television and internet facilities.

'Mr. Johnny bought us the hi-fi system,' Evelyn informed her, grinning as she added, 'So we can play his music.'

'Johnny who?' Ric's friend who owned the plane?

Evelyn looked surprised. 'You don't know him? Johnny Ellis? He's a very famous country and western singer.' Then she laughed. 'They call him Johnny Charm. And he is.'

'Oh, yes! I've never met him but I do know of him.'

In fact, Johnny Ellis was really big on the country and western scene, having made a huge hit in America with his songs. He was also something of a pin-up boy—a gorgeous hunk, while still exuding a very earthy hometown charm.

'Long time ago he and Mr. Ric were at Gundamurra together,' Evelyn ran on. 'Two of Mr. Patrick's boys. Now they are both famous. Mr. Johnny comes back here a lot. He says we are his inspiration.'

Hence the plane, Lara thought. And Johnny Ellis must also have been convicted of something criminal when he was a teenager, and given the same choice as Ric— *two of Mr. Patrick's boys.* Lara wondered how many of them there had been over the years, how many had made good after being here. *I'll make good, too,* she promised herself.

The one other room which fascinated her was the sewing room. 'Mrs. Maguire made everything here,' Evelyn explained. 'The curtains and cushion covers and patchwork quilts. Tablecloths and serviettes, too. Dresses for the girls. She loved making up patterns.'

There were bolts of fabric stacked against the wall, boxes galore containing samples of materials. The whole room was set up very professionally with a central table for cutting out, good lighting, shelves of cotton reels in every shade of colour, a range of scissors.

'Do any of her daughters sew?' Lara asked.

'Not much. Only to fix things. The oldest one, Miss Jessie, has just become a doctor. She wants to work for The Royal Doctor Flying Service. Miss Emily is a helicopter pilot and does mustering up north. Always loved flying. The youngest one, Miss Megan, is studying at an agricultural college. I think she aims to take over from Mister Patrick and run Gundamurra.'

A woman...running this vast sheep station?

Why not?

Lara berated herself for her own limited thinking. Clearly Patrick Maguire's daughters were all determined achievers. She herself had never nurtured any ambition. Modelling had more or less happened to her. At seventeen she'd been *spotted* at a pop concert, approached by an agent for a model company and very quickly promoted into the international scene, much to the delight of her mother who had pushed the career with so much pride and enthusiasm, Lara hadn't considered anything else.

By the time she'd met Gary she had tired of the scene, the constant travelling, the long exhausting photographic sessions, the sense of always being on show, the clothes that were more bizarre display pieces than actually wearable in real life. Everything was a performance and she'd yearned to feel more grounded.

Getting married and having a family had felt the right step to take. Maybe working in a kind of dream factory had seriously impaired her judgment. Certainly the dream husband had set about crushing her illusions very quickly and becoming a part of *his* family had shown her that having babies was not the answer to anything.

She needed to do something productive with her own life, not just reflect or enhance what others did or wanted for themselves. All she'd been was a show pony.

There was no sense of self-worth in that. Ric had given her the time and space to sort herself out while she was here, and this purpose was very much on her mind when Evelyn finally ushered her into Patrick's office.

He gave her a benevolent smile and invited her to sit down—this man who'd fathered three daughters now carving out their own paths in life—who'd been the father figure to boys who'd gone off the rails, setting them on their feet to go forward with confidence in their abilities to make something positive of their future. She saw kindness in his eyes, but knew there was a lot more than kindness in this man's make-up. He had to have a very shrewd knowledge of human nature and how it could be best put to work.

'You look better this morning,' he started.

Less beaten, she thought, determined on rising from the wretched ashes of her marriage to Gary Chappel. 'I won't let Ric down,' she said firmly.

Patrick frowned, gesturing a dismissal of her reply. 'I understand you're grateful to Ric, but Lara…don't hang what you do here on him. Ric wouldn't want you to measure this time by what he or anyone else might expect of you. It's your time. Make it belong to you, doing what you want because *you* want it.'

The slow, serious words struck a realisation that she'd spent far too many years pleasing others, firstly in a desire for their approval, then because if she didn't please, it meant getting hurt.

Clearly, Patrick Maguire was very different to her own father who'd had the habit of laying down the law with dictatorial impatience for any argument whatsoever. He'd never *listened* to her. She suspected he'd approved her modelling career and marriage because in his view, women were meant to look beautiful and marry well.

Full stop. They weren't supposed to think or quarrel with the men who were in charge of them.

Even though he was paralysed by a stroke and cared for in a nursing home, her mother was still subservient to him. Her reply to everything Lara had told her was, 'Your father wouldn't have wanted...'

Always your father...your father...your father....

Lara's cry, 'What about me?' had never been heeded.

Eyeing Patrick curiously, she asked, 'Is this what you tell the boys who've come here? To shed the influences that have led them into trouble?'

'That's quite a leap,' he said appreciatively, settling back in the big leather chair behind his working desk—a man who was comfortable with himself, not needing to impress, yet all the more impressive because of it. His eyes twinkled. 'What did Ric tell you about his time here?'

'Not much. He explained the program you ran as an alternative to spending time in a detention centre. And when he spoke of you it was with enormous respect and trust.'

He nodded, a musing little smile softening his expression. 'Some boys responded to the challenge. Others just put in their time. Ric, Johnny and Mitch were like the three musketeers, determined to fight their way out of where they were.'

'Mitch, too?' Lara looked her surprise and confusion. 'I didn't think anyone with a criminal record could go into law.'

'Mitch was a special case. He didn't defend himself at the time. There were extenuating circumstances that were eventually put before the court.'

'Through your connections?'

'Yes and no.' He shrugged. 'Because of my program here I was listened to, but the outcome of the hearing depended on what Mitch put forward himself.'

Not a backroom power play. Lara was relieved to hear it. She didn't want to think of Patrick Maguire doing the kind of deals she knew Victor and Gary did—bribing their way to the outcome they wanted. She needed to know Mitch Tyler was straight, too, not dependent on others' influence.

'Don't worry about Mitch, Lara.' Patrick's smile had a touch of whimsy in its tilt. 'Justice is a burning issue to him. Always was. One way or another, he'll checkmate Gary Chappel.'

Lara wondered if her thoughts were transparent. Not that it mattered. She had her answer. 'Has there been…any news… this morning?'

He shook his head. 'Maybe tonight.'

Lara hoped Kathryn was safe.

Patrick shifted, leaning forward, resting his arms on the desk, regarding her with lively curiosity. 'I've always asked each boy who chose to come to Gundamurra…what would he like to have that would add personal pleasure to his time here?' He paused a moment, then softly asked, 'Is there something you would like, Lara?'

She hadn't thought about her own personal pleasure for a very long time. Even last night with Ric, wanting him...it had all been focused on what he could *give* her, not what she could give herself. Apart from undoing his shirt buttons, she had been more passive than active...letting it happen to her. That seemed to be the story of her life.

'What did Ric choose?' she asked.

'A camera.'

'Johnny?'

'A guitar.'

'And Mitch?'

'A chess set.'

They had known what they wanted. Why didn't she? Was she just a blob to be directed by others, having no direction of her own?

'You don't have to answer straightaway, Lara,' Patrick said kindly. 'Think about it. Let me know when…'

'There is something I'd like to try,' she burst out, liking the idea as it had raced into her mind. 'Evelyn showed me the sewing room. She said no one uses what's there anymore…all the different fabrics and cottons. Maybe I could design and make things…if you wouldn't mind.' She flushed as she realised she might be treading on private ground.

'My wife would have been pleased to share her hobby with another woman,' he said with warm encouragement. 'Please feel free to use whatever's in the sewing room.'

'Thank you.'

'You're welcome.' He pushed up from his chair, rising to his full formidable height. 'Now let me walk you around the station…meet the other women…get your bearings.'

Yes, Lara thought, she needed to get her bearings very straight in her mind, not for her new environment so much as for her own life. No one ever really got a clean new slate, but this, she decided, was as good a chance as she was ever likely to have. It was up to her to make the most of it.

CHAPTER NINE

FOR three long months Ric had been moving around—Los Angeles, New York, London—going about his business, being alert for any trouble. As far as he knew there was none, not even with his Sydney office where Kathryn was still operating without any further problems. To his mind, Mitch had successfully quashed any move by Gary Chappel to raise more hell for Lara or anyone connected to her.

It was safe for him to go home.

He'd take every precaution not to be followed to Gundamurra. He was sure he could do it without endangering Lara. The desire—the need—to be with her again, to assure himself that everything was fine between them, had been building to such a pitch, he could barely concentrate on anything else.

For the past few weeks he'd been feeling something was wrong. When he'd first set up the private Internet site for them to correspond with absolute safety, Lara's messages had been like a daily diary, nothing deeply personal but full of her activities and written in an enthusiastic vein. He'd been satisfied she wasn't fretting and was communicating in a natural open way that he found very reassuring.

More recently her messages had tapered off into flat little reports. Maybe it was simply that the newness of her life on an Outback station had worn off. It wasn't surprising or adventurous or exciting anymore. Yet he sensed a depression that worried him, spurring him to act.

Gundamurra might not be the right place for her. He could bring her to London, watch over her himself. There were dozens of alternatives. All he needed was her compliance and he'd take her anywhere.

The first step was to talk to her, face-to-face, and that meant flying home. He'd written his intention of visiting Gundamurra last night. Her reply had to come this morning. He didn't want to leave his Knightsbridge apartment until it did. Impossible to set his mind to working in his London office today.

He forced himself to have some breakfast then checked his home computer again.

Yes…a message.

Ric stared at the monitor screen, feeling his heart squeeze into a painfully tight ball as he read Lara's reply over and over again, desperately trying to interpret it differently to what it said only too plainly.

It's better for me if you don't come, Ric.

No explanation.

Just the one line.

And his knotted gut was telling him it was because he'd had sex with her and she

didn't want to be reminded of it. Didn't
want him thinking it could be on again.
Didn't want the hassle of a confrontation
about it.

Mistake.

Huge mistake.

And he couldn't undo it.

So what the hell was his next step?

Ric pushed himself away from the computer with its dead-end message, refusing
to believe he had no future with Lara. The
connection between them had been too real,
too strong. There had to be a way over this
barrier.

He paced around his apartment, burning
off the negative energy that pressed in on
him—the old defeatism that had kept him
away from her in the past. He *was* good for
her. She'd wanted him to make love. And
she couldn't now think of it as a bad experience. It had been great for both of them.
He couldn't be mistaken about that.

Perhaps she was now ashamed of having had that need at the time. Linking him to Gary. Having had months of freedom to sort out what she wanted, she might well have developed a desire to be free of attachment to any man—an easier life, not complicated by relationships where more could be expected of her than she was willing to give. The short reports might mean she'd been weaning herself off any sense of dependence on him, subtly letting him know that maintaining a rapport with him held less and less importance.

A phase of detachment was not unreasonable in the circumstances. It meant more waiting, patience on his part. On the other hand, surely she knew he wouldn't do anything to hurt her. So why block him out?

Better for me if you don't come.

Did she feel *safer* with him away? Was the fear of Gary still uppermost in her mind? Had something happened he didn't know about?

Ric snatched up the telephone and called Mitch at home, where he should be since it was now well into the evening in Australia. The call was promptly answered by his old friend, much to Ric's relief.

'Is there any pressing reason why I shouldn't come home?' he blurted out.

Mitch weighed the question for a few moments, then replied, 'None that I know of, providing you exercise due care.'

'There's no overt threat from the Chappel front? Something that's worrying Lara?'

'All quiet there. Certainly Victor Chappel accepts there will be a divorce. I don't trust Gary not to seize any chance he can get to stop it so I would empha-sise...don't lead him to Lara.'

'I can use Johnny's plane again to fly to Gundamurra.'

'That would be the best way if you *must* go, Ric.'

'You don't think I should?'

Another longer pause. 'It's not for me to judge. I've never seen the two of you together…'

'But…?' Ric pressed.

'Lara has been through a lot. More than you know, Ric, and I'm not at liberty to tell you.'

'You're saying my presence might be an unwelcome pressure.'

'I don't know. I do know that for other women who've been in a similar situation…it's not forgotten in three months. It's a long, uphill battle to put it behind them.'

Time…

As much as Ric wanted to leap over it, he couldn't ignore Mitch's advice nor Lara's own words. He resigned himself to more months of patience, ended the call to Mitch and went back to his computer. His fingers tapped out the message—

As you wish, Lara.

*   *   *

As you wish…

Tears welled into Lara's eyes as she stared at the words Ric had written back to her…giving words…so typical of everything he'd done for her…giving…

Yet his caring for her needs only added another burden to her torment. She'd asked too much of him and now she was damned for it.

Three months' pregnant…

Lara propped her elbows on the computer desk, buried her face in her hands and wept.

Outside the heavens opened again and dropped another load of drenching rain. It drummed on the tin roof of the homestead, drowning out the sound of her private grief. Not that anyone would be listening. Patrick had set aside this time in the office for her use. She was always left alone to write to Ric.

But how could she continue this link with him?

If the baby was Gary's…there would be no escaping the Chappel family, even with a divorce. She'd thought wildly of somehow arranging an abortion but she couldn't bring herself to go down that dark road, not having had a stillborn child. It was her baby, too. Every innocent life was precious.

And it might be Ric's child…a desperate hope that would at least save her from being connected to Gary again, yet dreadfully unfair to Ric, trapping him into fatherhood, giving him no choice about it.

Guilt writhed through her. How could Ric ever trust her word again? She'd let him believe that the contraceptive pill she'd been taking would protect her from pregnancy, recklessly pressing him into making love to her. He wouldn't have gone through with it otherwise. She had used him to drive Gary out of her mind—wantonly used him—not caring about anything but her own selfish needs.

The sheer dishonesty of it sickened her. It would surely sicken him, too. She couldn't even face him with the possibility that the child was his. The shame was too great.

No...she had to assume it was Gary's...live with the consequences...end the link with Ric now. It was the only fair thing to do. This wasn't his problem. It was hers and hers alone.

No forcing herself to write cheerful little messages to him. That was dishonest, too. She pulled herself together, stabbed a finger at the switch on the monitor screen, watched *As you wish, Lara* wink out into blank darkness, then shut the computer down.

It wasn't what she wished.

But there was no turning back the clock.

She left the office and stood on the veranda, watching the rain come down—almost blinding sheets of it. There'd been storms like this for the past few days, causing the river to rise, bringing the danger of flooding. All the men were working hard, moving the stock to safe paddocks. It had to be done by horseback. The ground had become too boggy for any motorised vehicles.

She knew everything about the life here now. It had a natural harmony that she liked. And there was nothing pretentious about the people on the station. What you saw was what you got. No hidden agendas.

She was the only person hiding something.

So far she'd managed to keep her pregnancy to herself. The loose shirts she wore covered her thickening waistline, and as with her last pregnancy, she didn't suffer bad morning sickness. No throwing up. Mostly the nausea receded when she ate something. And since she spent afternoons in the sewing room, it was easy to take a little nap there so no one knew of the fatigue that sometimes overwhelmed her.

She might be able to go another month before the truth was too obvious to hide any longer. What then? Sooner or later she would have to tell Patrick. Would he let her stay here? Have the baby here?

Would she have to tell Mitch Tyler, too?

A baby couldn't be kept a secret forever.

Ric would inevitably learn of it, one way or another…and he'd feel betrayed.

She was no good for him.

She'd never been good for him.

And there was no chance of redemption now.

No sunshine after the rain.

She took her misery to bed and listened to the constant beat of the rain on the roof, wanting it to beat out any more thought. Yet she kept hearing…

As you wish…as you wish…as you wish…

Back in Sydney, Gary Chappel was getting what *he'd* wished for…the mistake from

Ric Donato that would lead him to his run-away wife. He'd paid through the nose for it, but his private investigator had finally come up with the goods from the illegal tap on Mitch Tyler's home telephone.

Gundamurra.

CHAPTER TEN

THE sound of a plane coming in woke Lara from her midafternoon nap. Ric, she thought, her heart kicking with instant apprehension. Had he changed his mind and come after all? But surely he would have let Patrick know of his intention. And he couldn't have got here this fast...could he?

He'd been in London three nights ago.

And he'd written, 'As you wish.'

Reason fought off the rush of frantic worry. No one could land, anyway. The airstrip wasn't firm enough after all the rain they'd had. Only a helicopter could make a safe landing and this was not the sound of a helicopter. But the pilot was flying very low.

Someone in trouble?

She was up and running.

170

People were yelling, 'It's coming down.'

Outside the homestead, it seemed everyone was running, knowing instinctively that help might be needed. They all saw it happen and could do nothing to stop it. The landing gear ploughed into the soggy ground. The nose of the plane went down. The tail flipped.

The shock of the crash stopped Lara in her tracks. Waves of nausea rolled through her. Frightened of fainting, she managed to stumble to a bench seat under one of the pepper trees and lowered her head to below her knees, trying to fight off the dizziness. Evelyn found her there and hauled her back to the kitchen, sitting her down at the table and making her a cup of tea.

'It wasn't Johnny's Cessna, was it?' Lara pleaded.

'No. None of our neighbours either. Looked like a charter,' Evelyn answered bruskly. 'Someone lost, most likely, and not even having the sense to call us on the radio about the condition of the airstrip.'

'Maybe they couldn't. Or were too low on fuel to go anywhere else.'

'That's not for you to worry about. It's men's work down there.' Evelyn gave her a knowing look. 'You have to be looking after yourself, Miss Lara. I've seen too many pregnant women not to recognise the signs.'

Another shock.

'If you want to keep it to yourself, that's fine, but you might as well know you're not fooling me. Now drink up your tea and off to bed with you. That plane crash won't be any business of yours.'

Lara felt too weak to argue. She did as she was told, grateful to slip into bed and not have to involve herself with the horror at the airstrip.

Yet in the end it was her business.

Patrick came into her room, drew a chair up beside her bed and regarded her with a gravity that had her nerves twitching in alarm. Had Evelyn told him of her pregnancy? Should she confess it now? Or did he have bad news about the plane crash?

It couldn't have been Ric...could it? Why would he charter a plane when he could use Johnny's? Her mind whirled in a frenzy of stress as she waited for Patrick to speak.

'Lara...your husband was in that plane.'

Gary?

The shock of it rendered her speechless. Her stomach churned as fear swept past the shock. Gary had come for her. He'd found out she was at Gundamurra, chartered a plane and...everything within her shrank from having to confront him. Yet there was nowhere to hide now. He *knew*...

'He was not strapped into a seat,' Patrick went on. 'There was nothing we could do for him.'

What did he mean...there was nothing they could do for him? It was Gary who had the power, who'd do whatever was needed to get his own way.

'He's dead, Lara.'

Dead?

Gary…dead?

Powerless to do…anything at all?

'He died before we could get to him. The impact of the crash…'

Dead…

Gone…

He could never touch her again…never direct any part of her life again…or her baby's…it was as though God was having mercy on her by taking him away.

I'll be a good mother, she silently promised, her hand moving protectively to the slight mound that held the new life inside. If she achieved nothing else with this second chance to be free of fear, she would ensure her child would know only love from her, regardless of who the father was.

'The pilot and a third man—a private investigator—have multiple injuries,' Patrick said, letting her know Gary had come with a backup man.

No doubt if conditions had been favourable, she would have been abducted back to Sydney, put into one of the Chappel medical clinics, classed as a mental breakdown needing psychiatric attention, and once it was discovered she was pregnant...but that couldn't happen now.

'A rescue helicopter will be arriving soon to fly them to Bourke for treatment. Gary's body will also be going. I have to ask...' Patrick heaved a sigh and quietly added, '...do you want to see him, Lara?'

She shook her head.

'I thought...you might want to be sure.'

She swallowed hard and forced herself to ask, 'Is there any doubt?'

'He carried identification and the private investigator confirmed it. There's no cause for doubt. The police in Bourke can contact his father.'

'Then I don't need...to see him.'

'Only if you want to.'

'No.' Instant and decisive. Better to think of him as completely gone than to have some awful last image of him stamped on her mind.

Patrick nodded and rose to his feet. 'I'll have Evelyn sit with you. If there's anything you need or want, just tell her.'

'Thank you.'

She closed her eyes.

The hunt was over.

Ric was not in danger anymore.

Set free.

She had to set him free, too.

Raising the possibility of fatherhood would not be fair. Even if the child was his, the responsibility was all hers. It would be terribly wrong to hang a lifelong commitment on him when he would have chosen differently. He'd done so much to give her freedom. To lean on him any more...to take his freedom from him...

If this baby was the result of a lie...

Better that Ric didn't know.

A lie was the worst possible foundation for a lifelong relationship.

And she wanted her baby to know only love.

CHAPTER ELEVEN

RIC had come into the Sydney office to work because he couldn't stand his own company. It was four months since he'd seen Lara and the only communication he'd received from her this past month had been relayed through Mitch—a request for him to stay clear. There would inevitably be—and had been—a media furore surrounding Gary Chappel's death, funeral and inquest, and she didn't want Ric spotlighted as a player in her life.

No scandal for the gossip pages.

She had been legally separated from her husband, pending a divorce. Irreconcilable differences. No other man involved.

In short, Ric had been effectively sidelined with no comeback in sight. The respectable widow walked alone. She didn't need or want his support. Mitch had assigned her a good solicitor to handle Gary's estate and Lara had reached some private settlement with Victor Chappel so there'd be no contest. Ric suspected a deal had been made—her silence on the nature her marriage—no slur cast on his son's character—and she'd be a wealthy woman for life.

He'd felt increasingly savage about the hypocrisy of it all.

Even more so over being left out of Lara's life.

She didn't *owe* him anything. He'd told her that repeatedly. And meant it. Yet the intimacy they had shared...he couldn't accept that *it* could be just swept aside as though it was now irrelevant. No way could he forget the night he'd spent with her... how *right* it had felt...and her words about missing him all these years...

He was at the point of wondering whether that had been a seductive lie to push him into doing what she wanted—wipe Gary out of her mind. Yet he'd believed, at the time, it had turned into more than that—a mutual loving that had gone so deep he couldn't tear it out of his system, couldn't set it aside and go on as though it made no difference to his life.

It did.

'Ric…'

The insistent tone in Kathryn's call of his name broke into his turbulent brooding. His gaze snapped up, his eyes stabbing her with all the angry resentment he felt over the situation with Lara. She was sitting on the other side of his desk and he saw the startled look on her face, realised what he'd done and swiftly rearranged his expression.

'Sorry. You were saying?'

She grimaced. 'Have you heard anything I've said, Ric?'

'No,' he admitted, shrugging off any care about his lack of concentration. 'Better leave your report with me, Kathryn. I'll read it later. I'm not in the mood for discussing business right now.'

'Okay.' She stood up and handed him the stapled pages she'd been using as a reference. 'I'll be in my office. Call me if you want to question anything.'

He had a million questions, but not about business.

'Has Lara Chappel made any contact with you?' he shot at her.

She straightened up, her hands linking in front of her as though needing to guard herself from attack. Her eyes were wary as she gave a slow, measured reply. 'No personal contact, Ric. However, she did send me a beautiful arrangement of flowers on her return to Sydney, with a note thanking me for my assistance.'

Flowers for Kathryn.

At least *her* involvement in the rescue and its aftermath had not been ignored.

Yet this acknowledgment felt like an even bigger slap in the face for Ric. No flowers for him. *Nothing* for him.

Kathryn's hands started fretting at each other.

His tension was obviously getting to her. Ric was about to wave her on her way when he noticed something missing. 'You're not wearing your engagement ring.'

'I gave it back to Jeremy,' she stated flatly.

It momentarily distracted him from Lara. He frowned his concern. Rejection was hell. 'Your decision or his, Kathryn?'

'Mine.' Her mouth tilted into a wry little smile. 'He wasn't the man I thought he was.'

'I'm sorry.' The guy must have let her down in some serious way.

'Don't be. I made a mistake. Better to find out before I married him.'

'Yes,' Ric agreed mockingly. 'Mistakes can be very costly.'

Like making love to Lara.

'I've actually been seeing Mitch Tyler,' Kathryn said in a rush.

'You...and Mitch?' He was surprised.

She flushed and he realised she was embarrassed about telling him, yet there was a sympathy in her eyes which instantly had him writhing inside. Kathryn and Mitch...discussing him and Lara.

'Good luck to you,' he said bruskly and gestured for her to go.

As soon as the door closed behind her he was up and pacing, unable to contain the violent energy coursing through him. To hell with standing back and doing nothing! He needed action. He wanted answers. Lara's silence was killing him. He snatched up the telephone and stabbed out the numbers for the Vaucluse mansion.

Though how Lara could go back there was another question that taunted him.

But she had. Within three days of Gary Chappel's death she had flown away from Gundamurra—lifted out by a helicopter which had been paid for by Victor Chappel. A very swift return to the life she'd left behind in Sydney. Couldn't wipe the dust of the Outback off her feet fast enough. No waiting for Ric Donato to escort her anywhere. Not wanting him with her, not for love nor money. No need for *his* money now. As for love…

'The Chappel residence.'

Not *her* voice. Had she kept on the housekeeper Gary had employed? All the staff that had been *his* watchers, reporting on her? Ric couldn't comprehend what Lara was about anymore.

'It's Ric Donato,' he snapped. 'And I'd like to speak with Lara Chappel.'

A pause, then, 'Please wait, Mr. Donato.'

Waiting for what? Ric thought viciously. To be rejected point-blank?

At least that would be some satisfaction. He'd know exactly where he stood. Fantasy dead. Just another episode with Ric Donato put to rest. No *missing* him at all.

He waited.

And waited.

He was turning into stone while he waited.

'Hello, Ric.'

Her voice.

He could hardly believe his ears, having geared himself up to expect nothing. His mouth was completely dry. He had to work some moisture into it before he could reply.

'Lara...' His mind was blank. No other words came.

She broke the ensuing silence. 'It's good to hear from you.'

Good?

'I'm glad you feel that.' The remark flew out, edged with a sarcasm he instantly regretted. Maybe she had cogent reasons for not contacting him in person. Maybe she had cogent reasons for everything she'd done. If she was welcoming his call now... 'It's been a long time,' he quickly added.

'Yes. Yes it has.'

No apology. No excuse for her silence.

'I was wondering if we could meet,' Ric tested. 'Have dinner together.'

A long pause, then with what sounded like forced brightness, she answered, 'What about lunch? Tomorrow, if it suits you.'

Not dinner. Not risking a night with him. Not *wanting* a night with him.

'Lunch. Tomorrow,' he repeated, gripped by a fierce determination to see this through. 'That's fine. Where would you like me to take you?'

'No.' Strongly decisive. 'This is on me, Ric. I'll book a table at the Osiris Restaurant. It's in the Radisson Hotel, quite close to Circular Quay so it won't be far from your office. Let's say we meet there at twelve-thirty.'

'Twelve-thirty,' he repeated, hating the obvious limitations she was putting on their meeting. 'I'll look forward to it,' he grimly added, wondering if he was a stupid masochist, begging for more pain.

'Until tomorrow then,' she said briskly, and ended the call.

He heard the click of disconnection.

It felt like a shot in the heart.

But he would go tomorrow.

He needed to say goodbye to her—face-to-face!

Lara barely got the receiver down before she choked up completely, tears welling into her eyes, spilling down her cheeks. She tried to dash them away with her hands as she bolted upstairs to her bedroom, savagely wishing she didn't have to go through the wretched torment of meeting Ric tomorrow.

But how could she not?

He'd sounded hurt...bitter...and she felt deeply ashamed of the cowardice that had kept postponing any contact with him, evading a confrontation that would only be painful. She couldn't tell him the truth and didn't want to be put in the position where only more lies would effect the necessary parting. But an outright snub on the telephone...she hadn't been able to cut him like that. It was indecent, given all he'd done for her.

She reached her room, closed the door and leaned back against it, hugging herself tightly in a desperate attempt to reduce the ache of loss that had started up from just talking to him. How could she manage tomorrow...sitting down face-to-face...the memories of how it had been with him brought vividly to mind by his physical presence?

He'd cared about her.

Really cared.

Would he still care if she spilled out the truth?

Even if the baby wasn't his?

A terrible yearning for Ric to hold her again gripped her mind, her heart, her entire body. But that was precisely how she had got herself into this hopeless dilemma...being selfish. Blindly, foolishly selfish. Caring only for what *she* wanted.

So what could she say tomorrow?

Oh, by the way, Ric, I'm pregnant. Don't know if it's your baby or Gary's. Sorry about letting you think I was protected. I was wild for you at the time. But now it's come to this, how about standing by me for the rest of our lives? Love me, love my child, regardless of who the father is.

A great reward that would be for all his giving!

She'd made this bed.

It was wrong to even flirt with the temptation of asking Ric to share it with her, to take on the load of fatherhood when she'd led him to believe there was no chance of it.

No.

Somehow she had to make him believe she wanted to lead an independent life. That she had plans which didn't include him. In all decency, she had to thank him graciously for freeing her to pursue her own goals, and effectively bow out of any further connection with him.

But it shouldn't be a bitter end.

Hopefully an understood one.

Though her heart bled for all the things that would have to remain unsaid.

Her arms slid down to hug the child within. The shock of the plane crash and Gary's death had worried her. She'd returned to Sydney as soon as she felt well enough to travel, anxious to see a doctor and have the baby checked. So far everything was all right. Last week's ultra-scan had revealed a perfectly healthy baby.

She needed this baby to live.

Something good to hang on to.

Tomorrow she had to say goodbye to Ric.

And let him go.

CHAPTER TWELVE

Ric walked into the Radisson Hotel at twelve-fifteen. The entrance to the Osiris Restaurant was at one end of the lounge area in the foyer. He sat in an armchair which gave him a direct view of anyone arriving.

Taxis came and went on the street outside, unloading and picking up passengers. None of them was Lara. He tensed each time a chauffeured car pulled up, only to be disappointed when a stranger emerged from it. Time ticked on…past twelve-thirty, past twelve-thirty-five, past twelve-forty…

He wasn't paged to come to a telephone. No message explaining why she was late. After four months, any normal courtesy would demand punctuality for this meeting, or at least a call informing him of a delay.

Everyone had mobile telephones these days. There was no excuse for leaving him hanging.

Was it deliberate?

A message in itself—*You're not important to me*?

An even more demeaning thought occurred to Ric. He strode into the restaurant to check if a booking had been made. If not, he'd been kissed goodbye in one of the most contemptible ways imaginable. He'd pushed for some civility from Lara and she hadn't even granted him that.

'A table booked for Chappel?' Ric demanded of the maître d'.

'Mr. Donato?' the man inquired, as though *he* had a message to deliver.

Ric seethed at the thought that Lara had arranged to pay for his lunch while not appearing herself. 'Yes,' he snapped.

'This way, sir.'

He led off, leaving Ric little choice but to follow him. They were moving toward the far end of the restaurant. Ric quickly scanned the spaciously arranged tables ahead of them, not recognising any of the diners. His jaw clenched as he spotted an empty table tucked behind a buttress beside one of the picture windows. He was not going to stay here and eat alone.

But the table wasn't unoccupied.

Lara sat in the chair that was hidden from general view by the buttress, her gaze turned to the view of the city beyond the window. Ric barely had time to absorb the shock of seeing her before the maître d' announced his arrival, swinging her attention straight to him.

He'd seen many photographs of Lara since her return to Sydney but none of them had prepared him for seeing her in the flesh—the breathtaking beauty of her undamaged face. Her eyes were a stunning blue. Her skin glowed. Her gleaming fair hair was softly looped up, gathered into a sophisticated topknot, somehow accentuating the delicate perfection of her features and the graceful length of her neck.

'Ric…' She smiled at him, rose to her feet, offered her hand.

No moving out to give him a kiss of greeting, just a polite smile, more nervous than projecting warmth, and a hand which he took as he nodded and forced himself to return her name.

'Lara…'

He couldn't bring himself to smile. He'd never felt less like smiling in his life. She wore black. The grieving widow? It was a black trouser-suit, undoubtedly designer wear, the jacket fitting snugly around her breasts then flaring out into a feminine A-line, skimming her waist and floating around her hips.

He released her hand after a light squeeze and she promptly resumed her seat. The maître d' held out the chair opposite hers and Ric sat, too, his gaze falling on the pearls Lara wore around her neck, three strands of perfectly graduated pearls. Probably worth a fortune. Booty from Chappel's wealth.

Well, what did he expect? Ric savagely mocked himself. She wouldn't come to this classy restaurant in jeans and cotton shirt. He matched her appearance, anyway, even down to Gucci shoes. He just didn't like her wearing what Chappel money had obviously bought for her, keeping up the image of her high status marriage when both of them knew what that image had hidden.

'I was waiting for you in the hotel foyer,' he stated, looking her straight in the eye again, still resenting the long futile watching for her to show up.

'I'm sorry. I did say the restaurant, Ric. I arrived early and came straight in.'

'Very early,' he couldn't stop himself from commenting. She had to have been seated here for over three quarters of an hour by now.

She flushed and tried to shrug it off. 'I didn't want to be late. With traffic the way it is...'

'My mistake,' he quickly granted and tried to relax as a waiter spread the starched white linen table napkin over his lap and handed him menus for food and wine. 'Have you already seen these?' he asked Lara.

She nodded. He quickly made a selection, not caring what he ate or drank, just wanting the waiter to go away and leave them alone. Lara added her order and the business of the meal was done. He sat back and set his mind to taking stock of the situation. She'd come even earlier than he had. What did that mean? Anxious not to miss a minute with him or getting herself settled before having to confront him?

She looked calm, composed, still a touch of warm colour in her cheeks but her eyes were regarding him steadily, taking in every detail of his appearance as though matching it to her memory of him—a one day/ one night memory that she'd made no attempt to revisit until he had taken this initiative. So what was she thinking now?

'You look well, Lara,' he said, which was no more than the truth.

'I've been looking after myself,' she returned, instantly striking an independent stance. She didn't need *him* to do that for her anymore.

'Good!' he said approvingly, then bluntly asked. 'You don't mind living in the Vaucluse mansion? No bad memories crowding in?'

Again she flushed, her gaze dropping to the cutlery on the table. She moved it aside in an agitated manner, then pulled a glass of water toward her. 'It's a big house,' she said jerkily. 'And all Gary's stuff has been taken away. I only live in part of it.'

Her gaze lifted in a flash of determination. 'It will go on the market soon. An estate agent is already preparing for it to be auctioned. Until it's sold it needs to be maintained.'

'Of course,' he murmured, though he knew money could easily achieve that. The place didn't have to be lived in. His apartments were all regularly serviced while he was away.

She sipped the glass of water.

'Same housekeeper?' he asked.

'Yes.' She looked defiantly at him. 'I managed to hire Mrs. Keith again. She left the day after I did. I'd told Mitch Tyler she was one of the people who might testify against Gary and that did prove true. She's a good person and needs the employment.'

But another reminder of the past, Ric thought. Did Lara want that understanding of her marriage from the people around her? For what purpose?

'Do you have any plans for where you will go once the house sells?'

'I haven't had time to look yet.'

'But you've thought about it,' he prompted.

'Yes.' She shrugged. 'Somewhere smaller.' A wisp of a smile. 'A place to call my own.'

Another pointer to complete independence.

'In Sydney?'

She nodded and sipped again.

'Any suburb in particular?'

'I want to be reasonably close to my mother.'

Her mother? Who hadn't listened to her problems? Who'd sided with Gary?

Ric found his jaw clenching and it took considerable willpower to unclench it. Lara was choosing to be near people who hadn't lifted a finger to help her, while *he* had been kept out on the perimeter, barely acknowledged by her. It made no sense to him.

Unless he was the most painful reminder of all she had been through—the one closest to it because of the intimacy she had begged of him.

But what of the feelings that had surfaced that night?

Was she now embarrassed by them?

Wishing she hadn't laid herself quite so bare with him?

'Is everything going well with you, Ric?' she asked, assuming an expression of bright interest.

'Business-wise, yes. On a personal level...' His gaze locked onto hers, searching, questioning. '...I've been missing you, Lara.'

His choice of words were pointedly deliberate and she flinched from them, tearing her gaze from his and dropping it to the glass of water which she turned around and around on the table. He felt no sympathy whatsoever for her tension. If she'd lied to him about *missing him all these years,* she deserved to stew in her lie.

'Mitch Tyler assured me that Gary hadn't done you any injury, either personally or professionally,' she said stiffly.

'No. I guess you could say I did him one.'

It startled her into looking up, a pained confusion in her eyes. 'What injury?'

'I did take you from him,' he reminded her, returning a look of black irony.

'I went willingly. I'd already tried...'

'Yes, I know. But then it was also me who gave him the lead to Gundamurra, which ended in his death.'

'You? I don't understand.'

He shrugged. 'I guess Mitch didn't tell you that Gary's private investigator had bugged his home telephone.'

She shook her head.

'After you e-mailed me not to come, I called Mitch to ask if he knew of any reason why I shouldn't go to Gundamurra, with all due care taken. That's how your husband found out where you were, Lara.'

'Oh!'

'Though I daresay all's well that ends well,' Ric mocked. 'You're not only completely free of him now, but also left a wealthy widow.'

She took offence at the mercenary aspect. 'I'll only be taking what I need to…to…'

Ric waved a dismissive gesture. 'You're entitled, Lara. God knows what you put up with as his wife.'

'It's not about money,' she stated with fierce pride.

'No,' he agreed. 'You've already made it clear it's about independence.'

'And setting things right,' she quickly added.

'Oh?' He raised his eyebrows. 'Is that what this lunch is for…setting things right with me?'

She stared at him, through him, her eyes becoming unfocused. She finally dropped her gaze, shook her head, and muttered, 'I don't know how to do that, Ric.'

The wine waiter arrived with the bottle of Chardonnay Ric had selected. There was the usual process of showing him the label, uncorking the bottle, pouring a taster. Ric gave his approval. The waiter moved to pour Lara some of the wine. She covered her glass with her hand.

'None for me, thank you. I'll stick to water.'

Wanted to keep her head, Ric instantly thought, *while I lose mine.*

The waiter filled his glass and left.

Ric didn't touch it. He'd ordered the wine automatically—an appropriate complement to the seafood they'd selected. If he'd known he'd be drinking it alone, he wouldn't have even glanced at the wine list. Lara's refusal of it felt like another point of separation—one less thing shared.

Was he overreacting...reading this all wrong?

If he put himself out to be charming instead of challenging, would it make any difference?

She *had come* to this lunch.

He tried to push his anger and frustration aside, tried to come at the situation through her mind. 'I'm sorry.' He managed a self-deprecating smile. 'I'm not making this easy, am I?'

She sighed. Her eyes reflected a weariness of spirit that held out no hope for him. 'It never was going to be easy, Ric.'

Undoubtedly the reason why she had evaded—postponed—any personal contact with him. He decided he might as well be direct.

'Why, Lara? Is it because of that night?'

Again she flushed and couldn't hold his gaze, dropping hers to the glass of water again.

'I remember it as good,' he stated quietly.

She closed her eyes.

No reply.

The memory was very vivid in his mind...how she had responded to everything he'd done. Not once had he moved on without being certain it was what she wanted and welcomed. And afterward...the sense of loving and being loved. No hint of regret. No second thoughts about its rightness. She'd snuggled up to him and fallen asleep in his arms.

'I thought it was good for you, too,' he murmured.

She shook her head. 'It was wrong,' she blurted out. 'I shouldn't have asked. Shouldn't have pressed.'

Her tone was pained, carrying thousands of regrets.

Shame...guilt...humiliation...were all those negative feelings attached to him now, making it difficult for her to look him in the face?

'It didn't feel wrong to me, Lara,' he softly assured her. 'I don't think any less of you for wanting what you did. It's a natural impulse to use sex as an affirmation of life.'

'Please...' She raised anguished eyes. 'I'd rather you didn't refer to it, Ric.'

She was skewering him, giving him no room to move. He frowned, certain now that this was at the heart of the problem she had with being in his company. 'You want me to sit here and pretend it never happened?'

'I can't do that, either,' she cried, the calm composure she'd greeted him with now in total tatters. 'I'm sorry. You've been so good to me but...' Her eyes pleaded. '...I want to close the door on it, Ric.'

Wipe it out.

He'd made love to her because she'd wanted to wipe out Gary.

She didn't need that anymore.

Gary was dead.

But Ric Donato was still alive and kicking…kicking hard against her wish to wipe him out of her life. Futile…if she'd made up her mind.

'I guess you'd better spell that out to me, Lara. Do you only want the door closed on what we shared in the past? Or do you also want it closed on any future we might have together?'

She took a deep breath. Her eyes looked sick but she said the words. 'There is no future for us, Ric.'

It was a flat, unequivocal denial of the bond he'd felt with her—a bond that had spanned eighteen years for him and would probably haunt the rest of his life.

He couldn't stop himself from asking, 'Are you sure about that?'

'Yes. I'm sure.'

No hesitation. No room for doubt.

He should move. Go. Couldn't make himself do it. It felt as though every atom of energy had drained out of his body. He stared at the glass of wine the waiter had poured. A cup of poison, he thought.

'I'm sorry,' she murmured. 'I owe you so much and there's no way I can repay…'

His gaze flicked to hers in savage derision. 'There's no debt. Everything I did…was what I *wanted* to do.'

Her cheeks were burning. 'I kept all the dockets from the clothes you bought me. I've written you a cheque. At least let me repay that, Ric.'

She reached down for her handbag.

He exploded onto his feet. 'Don't!'

She snapped back up without the bag. He glowered down at the strained appeal on her face. 'This isn't about money,' he grated, trying to contain the mountain of emotion erupting inside him. 'It never was. Though I tried to close the gap between us by stealing the Porsche. That was the blindness of a boy who thought he wasn't good enough for you. I don't know what your measure is, Lara, but I will not accept being paid off.'

He had the grim satisfaction of seeing her look shattered.

'Enjoy your freedom,' he said.

And walked away.

CHAPTER THIRTEEN

RIC didn't go back to the office. He was in no mood to face Kathryn or anyone else. Having retrieved the Ferrari from the basement car park, he drove home to his Woolloomooloo apartment where no one would bother him.

The view of Sydney Harbour from the picture windows in his living room reminded him of Lara's view from the Vaucluse mansion. He'd barged into her life that morning—uninvited—and demanded that there be truth between them. Nothing hidden.

Was that why she couldn't live with him now?

Easier to hide?

Ric still couldn't get his mind around it. He told himself it was a futile exercise even trying to work it out. She'd stated categorically—no future together. There was no choice but to let her go. And that final insult, wanting to pay him...pointless to struggle for understanding when she clearly had no understanding of him.

The bond he'd felt had to be fantasy.

Time to close the door on it.

Get out of Sydney, too, right away from Lara.

New York. Things were always jumping in New York. A city where anything could happen. Easy enough to get back in the social swim there, maybe even find a woman who'd move him past Lara, give him a reality check.

He was reaching for the telephone to book a flight when it rang. He automatically snatched up the receiver, not remembering he didn't want to speak to anyone until he'd lifted it, and then it was too late. The voice of Johnny Ellis boomed into his ear.

'Hey, man! Glad I caught you some-where! Here I am in downtown Sydney with a night to spare before I fly home to Gundamurra. Any chance of you joining up with Mitch and me for dinner tonight?'

Ric hesitated, hating the thought of hav-ing to speak of Lara, knowing she would inevitably be brought up somewhere in their conversation. He'd borrowed Johnny's plane for her escape. Mitch had been privy to the whole affair, though that was mostly confidential. But not Ric's part in it.

On the other hand, be damned if he'd shut the door on an old friendship because of her! Mitch and Johnny had proved true over the years. He could always count on them. And the three of them didn't get to-gether much. Stupid to knock back this chance, letting Lara get in the way. Mitch and Johnny would still be figuring in his future, long after today.

'Sure, Johnny,' he answered strongly. 'That would be great. Have you got a res-taurant lined up?'

'I called the Italian joint you like, just below your apartment. Otto's. Eight o'clock okay?'

'Fine! Look forward to it.'

The boys from Gundamurra...

To Johnny it was *home,* the only place where he felt a real sense of belonging. Like Ric he had no family, and the two of them always went to Gundamurra for Christmas, Johnny visiting more often during the year. They'd been made to feel part of the Maguire family, welcome whenever they wanted to come.

Ric wished he hadn't taken Lara there now, though it had seemed the right place at the time—in fact, the only place which could have guaranteed her safe refuge. Even if Gary's plane hadn't crashed, Patrick would not have allowed Lara to be taken. But that was all academic now. The problem was, Ric knew he'd never be able to go there again without thinking of her.

Get over it, he savagely told himself.

He'd done the right thing in rescuing her from an abusive husband. What happened after that…well, it just hadn't worked out the way he wanted. Patrick had warned him of that, right from the beginning. So move on past it. You're a survivor, remember?

When he met up with Johnny and Mitch in Otto's that evening, Ric had managed to push Lara into a mental compartment with fortified walls. He ended up having to refer to her, as expected, but the emotion she'd stirred was safely contained. He brushed quickly over the whole issue, declaring it over and done with. Lara could resume her life. He could resume his. In fact, he was off to New York at the end of this week.

Mitch proved a ready ally in steering Johnny back to regaling them with tales of his music world and the evening was mostly filled with news of his most recent tour in the U.S., all amusingly told. Johnny had the knack of making fun out of everything. Ric even found himself laughing. No doubt the alcoholic haze of several bottles of great wine helped to relax him. And the company was good.

The next day he worked hard with Kathryn, tying up the managerial loose ends in the Sydney office. He'd be basing himself in New York for the next few months, flying out tomorrow afternoon. He wondered how Kathryn's new relationship with Mitch was working out but didn't ask. Personal business was personal business. Privately, he wished them both well. Good people.

The telephone in his apartment started ringing just as he opened the door. Frowning over who the caller might be—a glance at his watch showed six-fifteen—he kicked the door shut and strode quickly to the wall phone in the kitchen.

'Ric Donato,' he rapped out, wondering if Kathryn had thought of something he'd forgotten—more business to be attended to in the morning before he left.

'Johnny here, Ric.'

He was surprised. 'You didn't get to Gundamurra today?'

'Yes, I did. Flew in this afternoon. Sat in the kitchen with Evelyn while she fed me her carrot cake, freshly made and iced with cream cheese and walnuts.'

Ric smiled, picturing the scene. 'I trust you fully appreciated your welcome home.'

'Had three big slices. But that's not the point of this call, Ric.'

'What is?' Some problem at Gundamurra? Patrick not well?

'Well, I might be treading on sensitive ground here, but neither you nor Mitch mentioned it, and Patrick tells me he didn't know…'

'Know what?' Ric cut in impatiently, his gut contracting at the thought this might be something about Lara.

'I'm sorry if I'm out of line…'

'Get to the point, Johnny.'

A big breath. 'The point is…I remember that Lara Seymour was a big deal for you, Ric, and I figure, with all you did for her, getting her out of a bad marriage, bringing her here…well, I think you ought to know there could be a good reason why she didn't stick around for you to come and collect her after the guy got killed.'

'A reason,' Ric repeated flatly, fighting against rising to a bait that might give him false hope.

'Didn't make sense to me that she'd give you the flick,' came the painful remark. 'Anyway, I was chatting to Evelyn…'

Ric gritted his teeth. Of course, they would talk about him and Lara—the big drama on the station this year. He could see them sitting in the kitchen, eating carrot cake, tongues wagging between bites…

'Now you know nothing gets past Evelyn, Ric,' Johnny went on. 'And she told me straight-out that Lara was pregnant.'

Pregnant!

'Must have happened just before you got her away from her husband because Evelyn said she wasn't far along. Wasn't even showing—at least not obviously—when she left Gundamurra.'

Three months…four months now… seated at the restaurant, not wanting him to see her arrive…the loose jacket…not drinking any wine…

'Anyhow, Evelyn said the shock of the plane crash made Lara real sick. Looked like she was going to faint. Had to be put to bed. Evelyn was worried about the baby and she reckons Lara would have been, too, on account of her last baby had been still-born.'

Last baby?

Ric's mind was reeling. He hadn't known Lara had given birth to a stillborn child. But when had they had the chance to talk about such things? In the limited time they'd spent together, she hadn't wanted to discuss her marriage with him. Her subsequent e-mails had contained only news of what she was doing at Gundamurra. And the cheerful chattiness of those had started dwindling off...

When?

It hit him like a sledgehammer.

When she realised she had to be pregnant!

'Ric...are you there?' Worried tone.

He realised he'd stopped breathing and expelled the air caught in his lungs. 'Yes, I'm still here, Johnny.'

'Is this news to you?'

'Yes.'

'Okay. Well, Evelyn's guess is, Lara went back to Sydney as soon as she was well enough to travel because she wanted a medical check on the baby. Which all makes sense to me.'

And to Ric.

Devastating sense.

'She might be rid of the guy,' Johnny went on. 'But she's having his baby, Ric. Puts her in a bit of a dilemma, doesn't it?'

'You could say that,' Ric answered grimly.

Was it Gary's child? Did Lara know that with absolute certainty?

'Just thought you should have the full picture. Mitch said...well, never mind that.'

The two of them had shared a taxi from the restaurant last night. Obviously they'd shared more than a ride.

'Hope I haven't trod where I shouldn't,' Johnny added apologetically. 'But if it was me...I'd want to know the ins and outs of it.'

Ric didn't hold anything against his old friends. They cared about him. He'd thought he hadn't showed he was hurting, but...

'It's okay, Johnny. You're right. It's better to know. Thank you.'

'Hard call to make. Take care of yourself, Ric.'

'Will do,' he answered automatically.

Yet his world was now tilting to a very different angle. Ric knew, even as he put the receiver down, he wouldn't be flying off to New York tomorrow.

Lara was pregnant.

He'd used no protection that night.

She might well have lied about taking contraceptive pills.

If she could be pregnant to Gary in that time-frame, she could be pregnant to him, too.

Either way, Ric wasn't about to go anywhere without settling that question first.

CHAPTER FOURTEEN

LARA had turned the nanny's quarters, next to the nursery, into a sewing area. On the cutting table lay the squares of fabric she'd chosen for the patchwork quilt, all pretty prints in a variety of colours. A desperate need to block Ric Donato out of her mind had spurred her to spend most of yesterday arranging and rearranging the squares, trying to assess which combination would give her the most pleasing result. The quilt was to be only cot-size and Lara wanted it just right for her baby.

The ultra-scan had confirmed that her pregnancy was perfectly on the track. Amazing, seeing her baby on screen, being able to check that he or she was properly formed. Lara hadn't wanted to know whether it was a boy or girl. If something did go wrong—like last time—she was sure that knowing it was a son or daughter made the loss so much worse. Better to wait. Let it be a surprise.

Meeting Ric again had stirred up an aching desire for the child to be his. It had been so hard, sitting across from him in the restaurant, not telling him, feeling the blast of his anger and hurt, having to watch him walk out of her life.

It had left her quaking inside, agonising over whether she'd made the right decision. He had felt betrayed, anyhow. But, at least, this way, his involvement with her was something he could move past, free of any responsibility for what she herself had done.

All the same, she hoped the baby would look like him so she'd know. But if it didn't...well, it was her baby, anyway. And she had to get on with her life...without Ric.

Eyeing the quilt pattern on the table this morning, Lara decided she couldn't improve on it. The red border was right for it, too. Everything bright and beautiful. She gathered up the first row of squares and settled herself in front of the sewing machine, bought on her return to Sydney. During her months at Gundamurra, she'd found enormous pleasure in creating and making her own designs. She wanted to keep on with it, maybe develop a business later on.

The buzz of the machine blocked out any sounds from the rest of the house. This room was like a private little world—a world she'd take with her wherever she went after this house was sold. Ric had thought badly of her for staying on here, but the baby was her first concern. Best to move slowly, not get herself into a twist with decisions that made too many waves with the Chappel family.

Gary was gone. He couldn't hurt her anymore. And oddly enough, she felt sorry for

Victor, losing the son he'd groomed to take over from him. He'd laid out a program of settlement with her on the agreement that she didn't publicly blacken Gary's character. Having no wish to give any details of her marriage to the media, Lara had accepted Victor's plan with no argument at all, against the advice of her solicitor who'd insisted she was entitled to a bigger cut of the estate.

The extra money wasn't important.

Freedom with no comebacks was.

Once everything was legally wound up, she'd be free to go her own way, financially independent—if she was careful—for the rest of her life. Ric could scorn her for taking the money as much as he liked, but she wanted it for her child—backup security in case she wasn't successful in setting herself up in business. Besides, if Gary was the father, she was certainly entitled to it.

Having finished sewing the first row of squares together, she moved back to the table to lay them down and pick up the next row. Her attention was distracted by Mrs. Keith's voice, raised in protest, clearly speaking to someone else in the hall that led through this section of the house.

'I assure you, this is completely unnecessary!' She sounded upset.

Lara frowned, wondering who was overriding the housekeeper's sense of correct behaviour. Was it the real estate agent, insisting on some further inspection of the house?

The grimly determined voice that replied sent a whiplash through Lara's spine and thumped her heart into stopping dead.

'I will not be parked in some isolating room while Lara skips out a back door.'

Ric!

'Mrs. Chappel is a lady.' Outraged dignity.

'Who lies through her teeth,' came the fierce rejoinder. 'And if you're leading me astray, Mrs. Keith...'

'Don't you threaten me, Mr. Donato! Or Mrs. Chappel. I'll ring the police. It's only because you helped her before that I'm not on the phone to them right this minute.'

'Oh, I don't think Lara will want a fuss. In fact, I'm damned sure of it.'

'Well, we'll see what Mrs. Chappel says.'

The knock on her door kicked Lara out of her shocked paralysis. Her heart leapt into turbulent beating. She sucked in a quick breath. Her mind belatedly grasped that Ric thought she'd lied to him.

About what?

That was the big question!

She didn't have time to say, 'Come in.'

The door was thrust open.

'Mr. Donato…'

The shocked cry from Mrs. Keith was totally disregarded by Ric. He stepped inside the room, his savage gaze pinning Lara to where she stood by the table. The room seemed to flood with his anger, swirling around her in a storm of feeling that was just as quickly caught back, brought under control. She could see the effort it took him, his face tightening under the strain, his eyes glittering with fierce willpower.

He wouldn't physically hurt her.

Not Ric.

He never would.

But she knew he was hurting badly and she'd done it to him. Though she hadn't mean to. And somehow she had to make it better for him.

'It's all right, Mrs. Keith,' she assured the housekeeper, trying her utmost to make her voice come out with calm confidence. 'You can leave Mr. Donato here with me.'

'He wouldn't wait, Mrs. Chappel.'

Lara nodded to her. 'Don't worry about it. Please leave us alone now.'

With a disgruntled sigh, the housekeeper closed the door on them and left. Ric shifted to stand in front of it, deliberately blocking the exit from the room. His eyes

ran mockingly over the clothes she wore—
quite a dramatic change from the choice
she'd made for their meeting at the restaurant.

Lara's nerves twanged in alarm as his
gaze traversed her stomach. The stretch maternity jeans were comfortable around her
thickened waist and the loose flannelette
shirt hid the pot belly which was still small,
certainly not showing an obvious pregnancy. He couldn't see. He couldn't know,
she frantically assured herself.

He was probably thinking these were the
kind of clothes she'd worn at Gundamurra.
There hadn't been any need to keep up a
classy image at the Outback sheep station
and Lara didn't feel any need to change that
now. She wasn't going back to the socialite
life. The outfit she'd bought for their lunch
meeting had been like a coat of armour, de-
flecting any sense of how vulnerable she'd
felt inside. Better for Ric to think she didn't

need him for anything. Though that, too, was a lie.

Yet how did he know she'd been lying to him?

His roving gaze returned to hers, still with a hard mocking gleam. 'Have you told Victor Chappel you're carrying his grand-child?'

The words were shot at her like bullets, shredding her defences. She didn't reply. Couldn't. The shock was too great. She stared back at him in a helpless daze, trying to absorb the fact that her attempt to hide the truth from Ric Donato was now a totally lost cause. He knew. He wouldn't be acting like this if he was only guessing.

'Is that why you're still living here, Lara...playing the bereaved widow... making deals with your father-in-law... keeping him sweet so your child will have the chance of inheriting the lot?'

'No!' she cried, appalled that he should think her so calculating and mercenary.

'Then why hide your pregnancy from me?'

She could see how damning that was in his eyes. But the rest of it wasn't true. She shook her head. 'I haven't told Victor. I haven't told anyone. Only my doctor and he has a private practice, not attached to any of the Chappel medical clinics.'

'So...you're worried that the child might look like me,' he shot back at her. 'That would upset the applecart, wouldn't it?'

Lara felt herself shrivelling under the blast of his contempt. She had to swallow hard to work some moisture into her dry mouth. 'I wasn't going to claim Gary as the father,' she stated, but it came out shakily and Ric instantly pounced on it.

'Just let it be assumed...if there are no telltale pointers to me.'

She lifted her hands pleadingly. 'Gary could be the father, Ric. The night before you came to help me escape from him...' She stopped, flushing painfully as shame and guilt washed through her, seeing the sharp leap of realisation in Ric's eyes that this was what she'd wanted him to wipe out.

'You didn't want Gary to win,' he said flatly, recalling and repeating *her* words, damning her even further.

But that time with Ric had turned into much more. She desperately needed to tell him so and have him believe her, yet the words choked in her throat, strangled by all her actions since.

'So what was the plan, Lara?' he tossed at her derisively. 'To confuse the issue if you *had* fallen pregnant to Gary before you gave yourself to me? Say the baby was mine and not his?' He threw up his hands in disgust and moved to the end the table, pressing his balled fists onto it as he leaned toward her in biting challenge, 'Did you really imagine you could get away with that when DNA testing can prove paternity either way?'

'I didn't have a plan,' she cried. 'I was just...reacting.'

'Lying to me about protection,' he bored in.

'I didn't want you to stop.'

'And you didn't care about *my* rights, did you? I was just there to be used.'

'No!'

'And now that Gary's dead, *he* can't use the child to stay in your life, so it doesn't make any difference to you who the father is.' He glared at her in towering fury. 'Does it, Lara?' One hand lifted and sliced the air in savage dismissal. 'You can waltz off and do what you like with the child, without any interference.'

She closed her eyes, unable to bear seeing the dreadful pain she had given him with her deceit. 'It's my responsibility, Ric,' was all she could say in her defence.

'Oh, I'm not disputing that, Lara. Look at me, damn you! Don't think you can shut me out now!'

She opened her eyes, feeling utterly help-less to fix what she'd done. To him it was all offensive. 'I don't know how to make it right,' she said hopelessly.

'The procedure from here is very sim-ple,' he blazed at her. 'We go to a doctor of my choice—not your doctor, Lara, be-cause I don't trust you anymore.'

She flinched. Even knowing she'd bro-ken trust with him, it hurt to be the object of such bitter mistrust. 'I didn't plan getting you to make love to me,' she protested, needing to fight at least that accusation.

He straightened up, a tall powerful man, intensely formidable in his wounded pride. 'You called me back to you on the veranda, Lara. I'd already passed your room.'

'I was afraid I might be asleep when you left in the morning. I wanted…'

'You wanted me to lie with you.' His eyes mocked any innocent spin she could put on that.

She shook her head. 'It just all built from what I felt with you,' she said defeatedly.

'Whatever you *felt* with me, Lara, it obviously wasn't enough for you to consider sharing your life with me.'

Her chin lifted, defying this judgment of her. 'Trapping you into it with a child...after I'd assured you I was protected? Would you be pleased with that situation, Ric?'

'*You* made all the decisions,' came the counterpunch. 'The queen...disregarding the pawn...as though I had no part in the game at all. And believe me...I will disappear from it altogether if it's Gary's child. But if it's mine...'

His jaw tightened. His eyes beamed hard, ruthless determination. '...don't think for one millisecond that I can be turned out of my child's life. I'll fight you with everything I've got for appropriate visiting rights.'

Visiting rights.

Of course.

He wouldn't want her after this.

His opinion of her was so low, it was a wonder he wasn't threatening to sue for custody of the child.

If it was his.

'Make what arrangements you like for the DNA test,' she said dully, resigning herself to the inevitable. 'Let me know and I'll be there.'

'Do I have your word on that?' he grimly demanded.

'Yes.' Her eyes did their own mocking. 'If my word is worth anything.'

He frowned, mistrust flitting over his face again. 'I'll line up an appointment. On the day, I'll come and collect you for it,' he said decisively.

'No need for you to suffer my company any more than you have to, Ric. I'll turn up for the test. I want to know, too.' She summoned up a wry little smile. 'I couldn't bring myself to ask it of you before. But now...' She shrugged. '...you've made your position clear. I can't keep you free of it any longer.'

'No, you can't,' he whipped back.

All her torment over the decisions she'd made had been in vain. Ric hated and despised her for taking the course she had ultimately chosen—the worst possible outcome.

'I guess we should both hope the child is Gary's,' she said bleakly. 'Then you won't have any need to be involved with me anymore.'

'You *want* the child to be Gary's?'

His intonation implied that such a wish should be anathema to her—wanting the child of a man who had abused her. Yet it was the one *out* for him, his only chance of being free from a lifelong commitment to a child he wouldn't have chosen to have.

'Don't *you* want that, Ric?'

His eyes flared with some violent emotion. When he spoke, it was with a bitter edge that cut into all she'd done wrong. 'You know something, Lara? You've never once asked me what I want. It's all been about what you want…which I've tried to give you. But I'm not giving any more. I'll do what's right for me. And I hope you'll have the decency to acknowledge what's right.'

She bowed her head, mortally ashamed of having taken so much from him and giving nothing in return. Though God knew she'd meant to…his freedom for hers. But he was never going to see it that way.

'I'll call you about the appointment,' he said bruskly.

And left.

Lara stared at the closed door for a long time, wishing she could open it again, do it all differently. Ric Donato had come back into her life—the one man who might have been her soul mate—and she had messed up the chance of their ever getting together in a happy and loving relationship.

She found herself fiercely hoping that the child was his. Then he wouldn't walk away. He'd claim visiting rights as the father and maybe somewhere down the line of the future they'd be forced to share, she might be able to change his opinion of her.

It all depended on the DNA test.

A knock on the door startled her. Her first thought was Ric had come back and she quickly called, 'Yes,' not caring if he berated her on some further issue. Any chance to correct his totally negative view of her was welcome, regardless of how painful it might be.

It was the housekeeper, returning to check on her. 'Are you all right, Mrs. Chappel?'

'Yes.' She managed a rueful smile. 'Sorry you were troubled, Mrs. Keith.'

The housekeeper frowned, not satisfied with having this matter brushed off. 'That Mr. Donato...he came in like a storm and

went out like one, too, not waiting for me
to show him the door.'

'It won't happen again, Mrs. Keith,' Lara
assured her, turning her attention to picking
up the next row of squares to show everything was back to normal.

It struck her that she was playing another
deceit, hiding the truth. Gary had taught her
to do that—maintain the image that nothing
was wrong or there'd be consequences she
wouldn't like. But she had no reason to
hide anything now.

'I'm pregnant,' she blurted out.

'Good heavens!'

The housekeeper's shock was testament
to how well Lara had hidden her true situation. At least, over the pregnancy. She
hadn't been able to completely hide how
Gary had conducted their marriage.

'Mr. Donato was upset because I hadn't
told him…and he has reason to believe the
child I'm carrying might be his.'

'Oh, my dear!' The shock melted into sympathy. 'Do you know…is it your husband's?'

Lara grimaced. 'It could be, Mrs. Keith. That's why…' She heaved a sigh that carried the whole miserable weight of her dilemma. 'Anyway, I've agreed to a DNA test to settle the question one way or another.'

The housekeeper nodded. 'It must be very difficult for you,' she said sadly. 'Can I bring you something? Tea and cake?'

'Yes. Thank you.'

Tea and cake…it reminded Lara of… *Evelyn!*

She hadn't asked Ric how he'd learnt of her pregnancy. *How* had been irrelevant when his very first words had expressed certain knowledge. While she had never actually admitted it to Evelyn, hadn't discussed her situation at all, there was no one else who could have been Ric's source on this.

Gundamurra...

Lara sank onto the chair in front of the sewing machine. Her gaze dropped to the squares of fabric she'd picked up and was still holding. Pieces of a pattern. At least she was in control of the quilt pattern. She wasn't sure she'd ever been in control of the pattern of her life.

At Gundamurra, she'd decided she would take responsibility for what she'd done, steer her own course, stick to what she thought was right, make her own way forward. But that decision had been tainted by the deceit it had forced her to maintain with Ric.

Deceit was never good. Even with the best of intentions, it was never good. Next time she met Ric...there might be only one more time if the child wasn't his. She crossed her hands over her stomach, closed her eyes and fervently prayed...

Please let it be his...please let it be...

CHAPTER FIFTEEN

LARA was already waiting in the obstetrician's rooms when Ric arrived. She looked up from reading a magazine as he entered, her gaze connecting directly with his, affirming that her word was good. She *had* turned up. In good time, too. It was still ten minutes short of the appointment he'd made.

Ric gave her a brief nod of acknowledgment as he strode to the receptionist's desk, his inner tension easing somewhat with the assurance of her presence here. Having had his name checked on the waiting list, he strolled over to the corner where Lara sat and settled on the bench seat adjacent to hers, not crowding her but close enough for them to speak privately.

Not that he had anything to say.

Sitting next to her was more a courtesy thing since they'd be seeing the obstetrician together. All the same, it was a mistake, making him aware of her in ways he needed to forget. He could even smell the perfume she was wearing, some insidiously floral scent that teased him into remembering the sweet sensuality of kissing her hair, her ears…

'Hello.'

The simple word of greeting from her, as though they were teenage kids again, had him gritting his teeth. She'd closed the magazine. Her eyes were fastened on him, eyes as blue as summer skies. He hated her…yet she could still get to him, making him want what they'd shared before… before he'd realised how she'd used him… and discarded him.

'Did you consider aborting this child?' he shot at her.

She flinched, but recovered quickly, her chin tilting up defiantly. 'No, I didn't.'

'If Gary hadn't died, it would have brought you trouble,' he tersely reminded her.

Pain in her eyes. 'I had a baby…just three months before you took me to Gundamurra. It was…stillborn. I couldn't take this baby's life, Ric. No matter what.'

'Fair enough,' he clipped out, and reached for a magazine from the coffee table in front of them, needing distraction from the way she was affecting him.

It was a fortnight since he'd rampaged into her house, forcing her to admit what he knew. He'd been so chewed up about her rejection of him—even as the father of her child—he'd been barely aware of anything else. Today was different. She'd submitted to his demand. And she was so stunningly beautiful, it hurt.

He flicked through the pages of the magazine but couldn't focus on reading. He kept remembering how her e-mail messages to him had tapered off into flat little reports on her life at Gundamurra, once she'd known she had to be pregnant. No doubt there'd been many conflicts in her mind. This past week, he'd been mad enough to think she might want to keep the baby because it could be his, but it really had nothing to do with him. It was obviously a maternal need.

'Losing a baby is a terrible thing, Ric,' she said quietly.

He didn't want to feel sympathy for her. 'Right!' he said, giving her a hard look. 'Then you understand I won't want to lose any child of *mine*.'

She nodded.

He saw her throat move convulsively.

Her voice was husky, her eyes filled with eloquent appeal as she blurted out, 'I'm sorry I didn't tell you.'

Was she? Ric stared at her, searching for some further layer of deceit.

'It wasn't because I didn't want you in my life,' she rushed out. 'It was because…it wasn't fair to tie you to a lifelong commitment when you would have chosen not to risk it.'

She looked sincere.

Ric frowned and returned his gaze to the opened pages of the magazine. He had no ready reply to what she'd said. Of course he'd been concerned about protection. A decent guy didn't just take a woman without caring about the consequences of sexual intimacy. Lara should not have lied about that. But…in all honesty…he hadn't wanted to stop. And given that moment again…if the truth had been told and she'd still urged him on…

'I had started taking contraceptive pills,' she added, an anxious pleading in her voice. 'Secretly, because Gary was determined on trying for another child and I didn't want it to happen, but I'd only been taking them for two weeks, so…I guess it was too soon for them to work.'

Was this another lie?

It certainly made sense that she wouldn't want to fall pregnant to Gary again—an unbreakable tie to him for life with the possibility of the child suffering abuse, as well. If she had been taking pills...even for a short time...he could understand her wanting them to be effective. Which would mean she hadn't told an out-and-out lie about being protected. More a desperate hope.

And the hope had died some six weeks into her stay at Gundamurra.

Maybe she'd been in such hell about it, she couldn't think straight...cutting him out because the child might be Gary's, and that would mean there was no ultimate escape from the man. Endless fear. And feeling she had no right to drag Ric into her hell.

He could accept that kind of reasoning. But once Gary was dead...no, he couldn't forgive her for cutting him out then. Paying him off...

'You should have wanted a DNA test, anyway,' he stated coldly. 'If the child was another man's, Gary wouldn't have had any lever to force an ongoing relationship.'

'Then he would have known I'd been with you,' she answered so quickly, it must have been played through her mind many times. 'He might have killed you...or had you killed,' she added grimly. 'Gary was very, very possessive.'

'But he ended up dead, Lara,' he shot back at her. 'And you still proceeded to push me away from you.'

Anguish in her eyes. Hot patches of colour burning in her cheeks. He wrenched his gaze from her and directed it firmly to the magazine.

'There's no point in this conversation,' he declared almost viciously, fighting the crazy impulse to sweep her up into his arms and promise everything was all right now.

It wasn't.

'If the results of the test prove the child is mine, we'll have something to talk about,' he added, deliberately limiting the focus of any further conversation with her.

The ensuing silence told him it had been effective.

Yet he couldn't stop himself from brooding over her attempts to clear up various pertinent issues with him. His mind kept returning to her claim that she didn't feel it was fair to tie him into a lifelong commitment when he hadn't chosen to risk having a child with her.

The fatherhood trap.

Except he would never have regarded it as a trap.

And she hadn't asked him.

Maybe because *she* didn't want to be trapped with another man. Which didn't say much for any positive feelings toward him. Yet…how could she have responded so positively when they'd made love if she didn't have good feelings with him, snuggling up so contentedly afterward?

The receptionist called their names.

Ric swiftly set the magazine aside and rose to his feet, instinctively moving to help Lara up, though she wasn't cumbersome with her pregnancy. In fact, the clothes she wore—a navy blue skirt and jacket, teamed with a smart overblouse in navy, white and red—disguised the fact she was pregnant at all, and she stood with the innate fluid grace he'd always associated with her.

Nevertheless, his hand stayed glued to her elbow as they were ushered into their meeting with the obstetrician, some latent sense of possession grabbing hold of his emotions, wanting her to be *his* Lara, the mother of *his* child. It was impossible to shake off the feeling that they did share a bond and somehow the child was a natural outcome of it.

Two chairs had been placed for them in front of the doctor's desk. The enforced separation helped Ric to concentrate on the purpose that had brought them here. The paternity testing was explained. Ric chose to give a small blood sample. Lara chose to do so, as well, but she also had to undergo a procedure called amniocentesis, where a needle was inserted through the abdominal wall to extract some amniotic fluid. This was necessary to perform cytogenic analysis. The tests on the samples usually took five days and the results would be express-couriered to both parties.

Once Ric's blood sample was taken, he waited outside for Lara's procedure to be completed, hoping she wouldn't be upset by it. A needle was just a needle. Nothing to worry about. But she might be super-sensitive about anything to do with the baby, having had a stillborn child. He didn't like the idea of her worrying about this one. Which led him into having a few worries himself.

Was she taking appropriate care?

Shouldn't she be bigger at four and a half months?

Was she eating properly?

What had *her* doctor said about the pregnancy?

Ric was champing at the bit by the time Lara emerged from the obstetrician's office. 'I'll drive you home,' he said, taking hold of her arm again and steering her through the waiting room.

'The fee...' She made a fluttery gesture toward the receptionist.

'I've paid it.' He gave her a searching look. 'Are you okay?'

She flushed, lashes sweeping down. 'Yes, of course. It was...nothing. Just a pinprick.'

'Some people get shaky about having needles. I'll see you safely home, Lara.'

She didn't protest.

He waited until he had her tucked into the passenger seat of the Ferrari and the car was moving before mentally pausing to take stock of where he wanted to go with Lara from here. He hated taking her back to the house that Chappel had bought, but it was her choice to stay there until it was sold. He found it bitterly ironic that the last time she'd been in this car, she'd trusted him to get her away from that bastard. Here he was, returning her to *the gilded prison,* possibly pregnant with her husband's child.

Though it might be his.

He *wanted* it to be his.

No denying that, whatever grief it might bring him.

'I presume you've had your pregnancy checked,' he tossed at her, keeping his eyes firmly planted on the road ahead.

'Yes. I've had an ultra-scan. There's no…no abnormality.'

'Everything's going well then?'

'The doctor says so.'

'Do you know the sex?'

'I didn't want to know. If something goes wrong…' She took a deep breath. 'Last time I knew it was a daughter. I'd even named her. She was already a person to me...'

Ric's hands tightened around the driving wheel. The sadness in her voice...the need to protect herself from more grief...she'd been through so much...it struck him he should have been taking far more into consideration than he had in judging and condemning her for pushing him away. A wounded animal holes up by itself, warding off friend and enemy alike, only seeing a world filled with pain.

'You have nothing to fear from me, Lara,' he said quietly. 'If the child is mine, I'll take a supportive role. I don't want there to be any conflict between us.'

She didn't reply.

A sideways glance caught her hands fretting at each other in her lap, revealing the depth of her inner tension.

'Lara?' he pressed, needing to satisfy himself that she was not regarding him as

a tyrant who would continually make demands on her. He wasn't like that. He'd be
reasonable, try to fit in with what she
wanted as best he could. Providing she was
reasonable, too. No way was he going to be
shut out of his son's or his daughter's life.
He'd had a rotten father himself. But he'd
be a good one, being there when he should,
giving love instead of abuse.

A heavy sigh signalled a dark weight on
Lara's heart. *'If the child is yours,'* she repeated in a flat, defeated tone. 'Yes, I expect you will take a supportive role, Ric,
given that you're the father. And no, I'm
not afraid of you.'

He could hear the line of logic left unsaid—no support at all if the child was
Gary's. She envisaged him walking out of
her life as abruptly as he had walked into
it. No future together.

Her previous actions had implied that
was what *she* had decided upon—for him
to be right out of her life. But he sensed

now it wasn't what she wanted. Or was he fooling himself?

It wasn't her fault if she was carrying Gary's child. No doubt it had been forced upon her. No choice. Though she had chosen *him* to wipe her husband out of her mind. How much did that mean?

'You won't mind my having visiting rights?' he asked warily.

Another sigh. 'No, I won't mind. I know you'd make a good father, Ric.'

But was he big enough to be a father to another man's child? A man he despised?

Either way, the baby was Lara's. She wanted it, no matter what. The critical question was...did she want him, putting aside everything else? Her previous rejection of him suggested that she didn't. Or that the whole situation was just too difficult for her to sort out. Easier to turn her back on it and go her own way. Which also meant he wasn't important enough for her to fight for. Or maybe she'd had a gutful of fighting in her marriage and couldn't summon the will to make another stand.

Ric found himself driving up to the front door of the Vaucluse mansion with this torment still raging in his mind. Lara bent forward, picked up her handbag from the floor near her feet, opened it, found the keys that would lock him out of her life again. Every muscle in his body tensed, aggression pumping through him. He braked more abruptly than he should have, the tyres of the Ferrari spraying gravel as they ground to a halt.

She waited for him to let her out of the car. He did it reluctantly, watching the silky fall of her hair flow forward as she ducked her head, stepping out. His gut was in knot. The urge to fight for this woman's love was like a madness in his brain, yet a vestige of sanity insisted it couldn't be forced. Love was either there or it wasn't.

He closed the car door and accompanied her up the steps to the colonnaded porch.

She said nothing. He said nothing. They stopped in front of the door. She looked down at the keys in her hand.

'Thank you for bringing me home, Ric,' she murmured. 'I guess...I guess this is goodbye...unless the DNA test proves you're the father.'

Her hesitant tone seemed to carry a sad yearning for a different outcome. It was encouragement enough for Ric to seize the moment and ask, 'Do you want it to be goodbye, Lara?'

Slowly, very slowly, her eyelashes lifted and the poignant feeling reflected in the beautiful blue eyes pierced his heart. 'I couldn't bear it...if you didn't care for my baby, Ric.'

There it was.

She shook her head, tore her gaze from his, inserted the key in the lock, opened the door, stepped inside and shut him out.

He'd hung everything on its being his child.

And it wasn't enough.

CHAPTER SIXTEEN

IT WAS the sixth day.

The obstetrician had said the tests usually took five days.

So today should bring the courier to her door.

As on every other morning, Lara doggedly went to the sewing room, determined on keeping busy, doing what she would have done if Ric had never learnt about her pregnancy. But she'd finished the cot quilt yesterday, and didn't have the heart to start something else, not when the courier could arrive at any minute.

She forced herself to sift through fabrics that might be good for cushion covers—a futile exercise. Her mind could not focus on anything other than the news she was waiting for—the news that would either bring Ric Donato back into her life or keep him out of it forever.

He'd cared about her, more than she had ever expected anyone would, and her heart bled over the loss of Ric's caring. She'd killed it by trying to set him free and he'd taken her decision as meaning it didn't matter to her. *He* didn't matter to her. And that was the biggest lie of all.

She left the sewing room and wandered listlessly into the nursery, stared at the newly finished quilt that was now spread over the cot, ready for her baby. The desire for it to be Ric's child was desperate now. She knew he would pour all his caring into being a good father, and maybe...maybe somewhere in the future, his caring for their child would spill over onto her and she'd feel it again...the feeling of being *his woman,* so special to him he'd do anything for her. As he had.

Tears blurred her eyes. There was no chance of any future with him if he wasn't the father. He'd made that all too clear. And she couldn't blame anyone but herself, hiding the truth, too ashamed to lay it all out to him. Too late when she did. Though he might never have accepted the child, anyway, if he wasn't the father.

She had to hang on to that thought.

It was her only protection from breaking up entirely. She had to stay strong for her baby, let Ric go if she had to.

'Mrs. Chappel...?' The housekeeper, not finding her in the sewing room.

'I'm in here, Mrs. Keith. Admiring my quilt,' she added in wry explanation.

The nursery door was open. Lara blinked hard to erase the film of moisture in her eyes and turned to face the housekeeper who took only a few moments to walk the extra metres along the hall. She appeared in the doorway, holding an official looking envelope, and Lara's heart instantly kicked into a fearful gallop.

'This has just come for you, Mrs. Chappel. I've signed for it.'

Signed…courier…it had to be…

Lara couldn't bring herself to move, to actually take it, knowing its contents would decide her future. Mrs. Keith had to enter the room to hand it to her, forcing an acceptance of it. The envelope hung between Lara's fingers and thumb, just a sliver of paper, yet it sent pins and needles over her entire body. She stared down at the official printing on its top left-hand corner—DNA Diagnostics Centre.

'Shall I bring your morning tea up here, Mrs. Chappel?'

She barely heard the words. Her ears were filled with the drumbeat of Fate rolling inexorably over her.

'No.' Even her own voice sounded far away. 'I'll have it out on the patio near the swimming pool, Mrs. Keith. Sit in the sun for a while.' Though it was unlikely to warm her. The chill in her bones went too deep.

The housekeeper nodded and left, giving Lara immediate privacy. Because she had to know what the envelope meant. Tea and sympathy, Lara thought, though nothing would be said. Mrs. Keith would wait to be told what could be expected in the future— a part-time father for the baby to be born...or none at all.

The question could be answered right now. All Lara had to do was open the envelope, read the results of the DNA test. Do it, she told herself, but her fingers wouldn't obey the order. They felt numb, not connected to her brain. Or there was a bank of resistance in her mind, overriding the dictate.

She walked downstairs and out to the patio, carrying the still sealed envelope with her. The sky was blue. Not a cloud in it. The harbour lay glittering in front of her. It could have been a summer's day, except for the slight nip in the air. But there was winter in her soul and the sunshine did nothing to dispel it.

She set the envelope on the table, where she had sat and wept when Ric had forced her to tell the truth about her marriage. He'd had to do that all along—forcing truth from her. Even now she couldn't look at it—the truth of the DNA test. After Mrs. Keith had served the tea, she told herself. Then she'd be alone with it, more ready to cope with whatever it meant to her.

The memory of Ric standing out here that first morning drew her over to where he had stood, taking in the view. Had he actually been looking at it, or seeing only the memories he had of her—memories of a far more innocent time when it had felt as though they'd been born for each other.

Even then she'd hidden the truth, avoiding telling her parents about Ric, knowing they would disapprove of any relationship with him and move to cut him out of her life. And that, in turn had led Ric into believing he wasn't good enough for her, stealing the Porsche...

It was she who wasn't good enough for him.

He'd grown into a man that any woman in the world would be proud to have at her side, and not just because he was handsome and wealthy. He was so much more than that...so much more. And she hadn't even had the wits to see through Gary Chappel's charming facade to the cold, cruelly calculating heart within.

She didn't deserve Ric, didn't deserve his caring. It was enough—more than enough—that he'd freed her from Gary so she could make something positive out of her life.

And taking her to Gundamurra. That had been good for her, too. She had a lot to be grateful for. Although none of it eased the ache inside her. She hugged herself, trying to make it go away. The baby would make up for the painful sense of loss. Her baby…

Footsteps on the patio behind her…the housekeeper bringing out a tray of morning tea things…the sealed envelope still on the table. What were Marie Antoinette's infamous words before she was condemned to the guillotine? *Let them eat cake*?

'Just set it down, thank you, Mrs. Keith,' Lara instructed without turning around. 'I'll serve myself when I'm ready.'

No reply.

No sound of the tray being set on the glass surface of the outdoors table.

No footsteps going away.

Absolute silence.

Was the housekeeper staring at the unopened envelope?

Well, at least it transmitted a message that Lara had nothing to talk about yet. Being the soul of discretion, Mrs. Keith would follow instructions and discreetly withdraw. Any moment now. Then it was up to Lara to face what had to be faced. No more hiding from it.

'You still don't know.'

The deep timbre of that voice—Ric's voice!—vibrated through every cell in Lara's body. Ric...here...! Dear God, did that mean...?

Her heart leapt with joy. A cocktail of hope fizzed through her mind. She swung around, giddy with the prospect of having Ric in her life on a continuing basis. He had to be the father of her baby. He wouldn't have come otherwise.

But his grim face made her check the burst of pleasure at seeing him. The dark velvet eyes burned like hard coals, and she felt their fire searing her soul, no quarter given in the search for a truth he was determined on having.

'I don't know, either,' he said, reaching inside his jacket and withdrawing the envelope that matched hers. He tossed it onto the table. It hadn't been opened.

Lara stared at it in shocked confusion. She didn't understand this. He'd wanted the proof of paternity, either way. Demanded it of her. It made no sense that he'd come here without first checking the results of the test. She wrenched her stunned gaze from the incontrovertible evidence that he hadn't, and forced it up to meet the blaze of purpose in his.

'Why, Ric?' she asked simply.

'Because you matter more, Lara,' came the heart-jolting reply. 'I would ac-cept...and love...any child of yours... because it's part of you.'

Love...her reeling mind clung to that one word. She couldn't quite take in the rest but she thought it meant he still cared about her, that she *was* special to him.

'The question is...' he went on slowly, searchingly '...am I deluding myself about what you feel for me?'

She couldn't speak. There was a massive lump of emotion blocking her throat. He moved toward her. It didn't occur to her to move toward him. Every atom of her energy was focused on watching him, trying to feel what he was feeling. The yearning inside her was so huge, she wasn't sure if she was misreading the same need in him...the need to have and to hold because despite all the differences between them— in the past and right now—they touched something in each other that blotted out the rest of the world.

Her hands were linked in front of her, instinctively protective of the baby in her womb. He gently drew them apart and lifted them to his shoulders. Her heart fluttered in wild hope. Everything inside her quivered at the sheer force of the desire he stirred.

'When we made love...' he murmured, his eyes softer now, molten liquid flowing into her, warming the blood in her veins, making it race to a chaotic beat. '...it was me, you wanted, wasn't it, Lara? Not just because I was there...and I could answer your need?'

Somehow she forced her voice to work. 'Only you could have done that, Ric,' she answered, and the truth of that night, which she'd kept dammed up inside her, burst its banks and came pouring out. 'And the need...the need was to have you. At least once in my life. Because I might lose you again. And I couldn't bear...not to have known you like that while I still could.'

He drew in a deep breath, his chest expanding with it. She could feel his tension in the rigid shoulder muscles, knew that what she'd said had hit him hard. But it was the truth and she fiercely willed him to believe her.

'It wasn't about...wiping out what Gary had done?'

'That, too,' she admitted. 'But I would have said anything to make you give me...what you did, Ric. I'm sorry it got so complicated...with the pregnancy.'

'It doesn't matter,' he said gruffly.

'It wasn't fair...'

He placed a silencing finger on her lips. 'There's nothing fair in love and war, Lara. We just have to survive the hard patches. And believe in what we're doing.'

The finger moved, trailing across her cheek, tracing its contours before shifting the fall of her hair back behind her ear. Lara stood mesmerised by its touch, feeling her skin come alive under the brush of his. It had always been this way with Ric—holding hands when they were teenagers... sharing that one kiss...the total experience of intimacy with him...

'I couldn't bear for you to be a battered wife,' he said softly. 'Not my Lara...'

His? Did he still think of her as his?

'You remained an unattainable dream to me until the day I saw that photo,' he went on, his voice furred with deep emotion. 'But what I feel for you now is very real. And if what you feel for me is real...'

The need in his eyes swelled the tidal wave of need rampaging through her. His hands cradled her face as his own came nearer and nearer. When his lips touched hers...covered them...moved them...the sweet bliss of connecting with him again triggered an overwhelming response. She kissed him back with all her heart, her soul, and her mind danced with the sheer joy of it...Ric wanting her, no matter what.

She loved this man. Loved all that he was. Her hands hugged his head, holding him to her. Her mouth expressed all the passion she felt for him. Her body strained against his, revelling in the closeness that was not going to be taken away. He was going to stay with her...love her...love her baby.

And in between the kisses his eyes shone down at hers, seeing, believing. It *was* real...this feeling they had together. He held her, his hands moving over her possessively, tenderly, lovingly, passionately, and the sunshine of his touch seeped into her bones, a brilliant heat that chased winter away.

'Come home with me, Lara,' he murmured. 'I need you to be with me.'

Not here with the shadows of her marriage. In a space they could own together. 'Yes,' she happily agreed, wanting what he wanted, yearning for it.

He smiled, drew back, took her hand. She looked down at this simplest form of being joined to him, remembering, feeling it again...the bond that seemed to link their lives to a magical place that belonged only to them.

'We used to walk like this,' she said, smiling back at him.

'I remember.'

'It's not a fantasy, Ric.'

'No. It's not.' He rubbed his thumb over her bare third finger. 'Will you wear my wedding ring, Lara?'

The breath caught in her throat momentarily. A kind of ecstatic incredulity billowed through her mind. So much...so soon? Yet the determined purpose that had brought him here still burned in his eyes, a simmering glow now, but telling her unequivocally the words were meant.

'I'd feel very honoured to wear it, Ric,' she said soberly.

'Then I think we should get married as soon as possible. Before the baby is born.'

'The baby...' Her gaze swung to the envelopes, still lying on the table. Her hand convulsively squeezed his as anxiety flooded through her. 'Ric, you have to know...'

'No. Leave it. I promise you it won't make any difference.'

'But it does. I haven't told Victor Chappel about my pregnancy, but if I have a baby who looks like Gary, or anyone in his family...' She shook her head worriedly. 'He won't let it go, Ric. And if you marry me, you'll be caught up in the fight, too.'

'Lara…your fight is my fight. I won't let you stand alone against Victor Chappel,' he said calmly.

'He won't give up. It will be ongoing…' The fear seized her brilliant bubble of happiness and started tearing it to shreds. 'He'll get some legal order preventing me from leaving the country with the child. Which wouldn't matter if I was on my own. But your business takes you overseas, Ric, and I wouldn't be able to accompany you. I won't go and leave…'

'The business can be run by others,' he argued. 'I can start something else.'

His confidence in resolving any and every problem soothed some of her agitation. But she couldn't help feeling it was asking too much of him. He hadn't lived with the Chappels as she had. Her gaze shifted to the envelopes again, drawn by a dreadful sense of inevitability that she'd bring trouble to Ric.

'Victor will insist on a DNA test, anyway,' she muttered. 'I have to know what I'm getting you into. I won't hide from this. I won't.' She lifted pleading eyes to his. 'If you want me to go forward with you, Ric, it has to be with the truth, both of us knowing what we'll be dealing with. That's fair, isn't it?'

He weighed her argument then slowly answered, 'As long as you understand I won't let you back out of marrying me, Lara. Whatever it takes for us to be together…I'm your man.'

Her man.

Yes, he was.

In every sense.

Whatever the future held, she would never undervalue his feeling for her, or hers for him.

'Thank you,' she said, acknowledging the extraordinary gift of his love. 'Thank you for coming back into my life. Thank you for rescuing me and making me feel like a worthwhile person. Thank you for letting me be one with you. I promise you I'll never turn away from that, Ric. No matter what.'

He drew a deep breath and gestured to the table. 'Then let's deal with the truth.'

She looked at the sealed envelopes. They held no power to hurt, she told herself. She and Ric had moved past that place. Determined to prove it, she stepped over to the table, picked up the closest envelope, tore it open, extracted the contents and read the results of the testing.

And it felt as though the world shifted.

All the conflicts she'd feared just... winked out of any possible existence. She looked at Ric—seeing him as the driving force behind everything that was now right for her. Even this. Especially this.

'It's you. You're the father of my baby.'

'Our baby,' he corrected her.

She laughed. And then she was crying. But they were happy tears, not tears to be hidden. Ric kissed them away and they smiled at each other.

'Come home with me now?' he asked.

'I am home with you, Ric. That's how it feels.'

'Yes. That's how it feels for me, too.'

CHAPTER SEVENTEEN

Christmas at Gundamurra...

R<small>IC</small> was looking forward to it.

'Got to show you off to Patrick,' he told the baby who was cradled in his arms, eyes closed, not so much as a flutter from the thick black lashes.

The rocking motion of the swing-lounge always did the trick—stopped the crying, put the baby to sleep. Ric automatically used his feet to keep the swing going as his gaze roved over the view from where he sat. To his mind, this deck outside the main living room was one of the best features of the house he'd bought for Lara. It faced north, catching the sun all winter, and the view over the bay at Balmoral with the Norfolk pines edging the beach and the marina full of yachts, coming and going, made sitting out here a constant pleasure.

Lara loved everything about the house and was still getting the furnishings *just right* for it, taking enormous delight in choosing exactly what she thought made it a home for them. It made Ric happy, simply to see her so happy. And Balmoral was just across the harbour from Circular Quay, not far at all for him to buzz into the office when he had to. Though he was taking time out for a while, enjoying being a father, giving himself paternity leave.

Right now it was his job to mind the baby while Lara and Mrs. Keith packed for the trip to Gundamurra. 'I'm a top-notch rocker, kid,' he told his charge whose perfect contentment confirmed the claim.

The self-indulgent boast brought Johnny to mind—king of rock when it came to country music. Ric grinned as he remembered Johnny rolling up to the hospital to view the new Donato, bringing his guitar with him, and singing the ballad he'd written about the boy from Gundamurra... 'His spirit would not rest...till he'd brought his woman home.'

There were many verses but that was the chorus, repeated so often, the whole hospital ward had ended up gathered outside Lara's room, listening to Johnny sing and joining in with him on those two lines. Totally embarrassing. But Lara had loved it. And Mitch had egged Johnny on to get the song recorded, give them all a copy of it for Christmas. No doubt Evelyn would love it too, play it endlessly, especially with having Gundamurra mentioned in the lyrics.

Patrick would smile.

Patrick...the only real father the three of them had ever known. Always there for them if they needed him for anything. Always coming through for them when asked.

'I'm going to be like him,' Ric promised his own child. 'You can count on me to plant your feet on the ground so you know how to choose your own path, get it right. And I'll always be there to back you up, lend a helping hand...'

He was glad he'd taken Lara to Gundamurra, that she'd spent those months with Patrick. Although she had established a better relationship with her mother, and even Ric was now acceptable to Andrea Seymour, there'd been no argument over where they'd go for Christmas. The Outback sheep station was now a special place for both of them.

It was going to be great this year. Mitch was coming, too, bringing Kathryn Ledger with him, which was certainly a sign that the relationship between them was getting serious. Though Mitch was a deep one. He didn't give much away. He might simply be taking Kathryn to Gundamurra to see how she reacted to it. A test. Mitch had a habit of cross-examining everything—a barrister by nature as well as by profession.

If it was a test, Ric hoped Kathryn would pass it. He liked her. Lara liked her, too. Though love was something else, as he well knew. If Johnny and Mitch ever got married, he wished for them the same kind of love he'd found with Lara. It made such a huge difference to his life.

'Mrs. Donato is ready for the baby now,' Mrs. Keith called out to him.

'Okay. We're coming,' Ric answered, pausing the swing-lounge and moving off it without a jolt.

The housekeeper was holding the door open for him to pass inside. She smiled at the two of them and he grinned back at her. 'Fast asleep,' he crowed, nodding down at the babe. 'See what a father's touch can do?'

She arched an amused eyebrow. 'Nothing to do with the swing, of course, Mr. Donato.'

'It's knowing the right rhythm, Mrs. Keith.'

'An instinctive knowledge,' she agreed, her eyes twinkling.

Definitely a good woman to have with the family, Ric thought. Lara had been right about that. A very helpful and pleasant presence in the house. Gave Lara support with the baby, as well, having had plenty of experience with her own children.

He walked through to the nursery where he knew Lara would be getting ready to feed the baby. She was laying out fresh clothes on the change table when he entered. She turned to him, smiling as she quickly unbuttoned her blouse and unhooked the maternity bra.

'We're all packed and ready to go. As soon as I've fed the baby, we can leave.'

'No big hurry,' he assured her. 'Johnny will wait for us.'

Her beautiful blue eyes sparkled with excitement. 'Just as well we're travelling in his private plane. I've got so many Christmas gifts to take.'

'This is the best one,' Ric said, smiling down at their son…Patrick Alexander Donato.

'And it's so right that he'll be spending his first Christmas at Gundamurra,' Lara happily declared.

'He won't remember it.'

'But *we* will. You've got your camera ready, haven't you?'

'Of course.'

'Then I know you'll capture it all brilliantly, Ric.'

She took their son who came instantly awake at the change of contact, snuffling around at the smell of milk. Barely one month old and latching onto Lara's breast the moment it was bared. *That's my boy,* Ric thought with fatuous pride, watching Lara settle into the rocking chair where she liked to feed him.

My son...my wife...our home...and Gundamurra for Christmas.

Life couldn't be better than this.

Except...he hoped they'd have a daughter next time, make up for the one Lara had lost. And he'd give her the pleasure of naming their little girl.

She'd insisted that he name their son— Patrick for the man who'd saved both of them, Alexander because the world was out there to be conquered—in a strictly personal sense. He was going to teach his son that barriers were only in his mind.

He and Lara could have been together a long time ago if he hadn't put that *unattainable* barrier in his own mind. Would have saved a lot of grief, too. But he couldn't redo the past, only make the most of the present and the future...the rest of their lives.

Lara looked up at him, her eyes softly glowing. 'I love our life together, Ric. Thank you for making it happen.'

'It could only happen with you. I love you, Lara. Always will.'

'It's the same for me. You do know that, don't you, Ric?'

No mistaking the love in her eyes.

'Yes, I know.'

His Lara...

Always had been...

Always would be.